DARK DREAMS

IN MY MIND'S EYE™
BOOK TWO

KELLI ROBYNS

MICHAEL ANDERLE

DON'T MISS OUR NEW RELEASES

Join the Florid Romance email list to be notified of new releases and special promotions (which happen often) by following this link:

https://floridromance.lmbpn.com/about/sign-up-for-our-newsletter/

Published by Florid Romance
an imprint of LMBPN Publishing
2375 E. Tropicana Avenue, Suite 8-305
Las Vegas, Nevada 89119 USA

Version 1.00, September 2025
eBook ISBN: 979-8-89354-947-8
Print ISBN: 979-8-89354-948-5

ONE

SMOKE AND AFTERSHOCKS

Ivy felt her pulse roaring in her ears as the paramedics rushed forward, flooding the candlelit darkness with strobing red and blue. The hooded man lay on his side in the grass, face turned away from the glow of the street-lamps. His tangled gray hair fanned around him like a halo. A pair of mourners stumbled back, giving the medics space. Ivy watched them kneel beside the body and begin CPR, but it was clear to anyone nearby that the man was gone.

She still felt the echo of his grip around her wrist, a phantom pressure that refused to leave her skin. His eyes had been milky and pale, as though he had stared into a world no one else could see. *You are not the first... and you are not the last.* She could still hear that rasping voice, so frail yet oddly forceful.

Ethan touched her shoulder gently. "Come on," he said in a low tone. "You're freezing out here."

Everything around them blurred, the sorrowful silence

of onlookers blending with the pulsing lights and the steady drone of sirens. Ivy nodded, unable to form words yet. She let Ethan guide her away from the wavering candles and the circle of stiff-lipped paramedics still trying and failing to bring the stranger back.

He led her across the street to a small cafe whose interior glimmered with string lights in the windows. A chalkboard sign out front promised espresso and fresh pastries, though it was well past the dinner hour. Ivy sank into one of the wooden chairs by the window, her gaze drifting to where the vigil still glowed in Dolores Park. The distance offered no comfort. She kept expecting the man to rise, to appear once more in that hood, telling her cryptic truths she could not decipher.

Ethan slid into the seat across from her. He hesitated before offering a hand, which she took. The warmth of his fingers wrapped around hers, grounding her. She tried to focus on the mundane details around them, the scuffed table, the overhead lights humming softly, the smell of roasted coffee beans. Ordinary anchors in a night riddled with shock.

A waitress approached, her face lined with worry. "You two all right?" she asked, her voice stifled as though she sensed something amiss.

Ethan nodded. "Just coffee, please." He glanced at Ivy, who managed a small nod. "Make it two," he added.

The waitress slid away to fill their order, leaving them in a silence interrupted only by the chatter of a few customers who looked too tired to care about the flurry of activity outside. Ivy swallowed tightly.

"He recognized me," she said at last. Her voice sounded distant, like it belonged to someone else. "The way he grabbed my wrist, it was so deliberate. Like he'd been waiting for me."

Ethan's eyes rested on her face. "What did he say exactly?"

Her throat constricted. She forced the words out. *That I'm not the first, and I'm not the last.* The memory sent a ripple of unease through her body. "It felt like a warning."

He gently squeezed her hand, then reached into his jacket pocket. Out came a cream-colored envelope sealed with wax. Ivy stared at it, recalling the chill that swept through her when he first showed it to her in the park. The same archaic seal, the same thick paper, the same sense of looming mystery.

Ethan's voice dropped low. "I opened this while I was looking for you. Inside is that name again." He leaned forward, lowering his voice. "*Lucien Grey.*"

The name spilled onto the worn tabletop like a living thing. Ivy inhaled sharply. She had seen it scrawled beneath that strange charcoal portrait hidden under her parents' floorboards. Lucien Grey had haunted her sketches as a child, a name she should never have known so young. Now it surfaced again, linked to a dead man's last words.

Ethan lifted the envelope and slid it across to her, letting her see the handwritten scrawl. He traced one finger over the lines of ink. "Do you know him?" he asked softly, studying her eyes.

Ivy barely breathed. She remembered the face she had

once etched, the angular cheekbones and half-smiling mouth she couldn't possibly have imagined at age six. Her pulse lurched. "Only from dreams," she whispered. "Until recently, I thought maybe I made him up. Maybe it was just some childhood nightmare." She inhaled a trembling breath. "I don't think it's pretend anymore."

The coffees arrived with quiet efficiency. The waitress set them down and slipped away again, her eyes darting with mild curiosity toward the envelope. Neither Ivy nor Ethan touched the mugs, their focus firmly on the unsettling message.

Ethan flipped open his laptop. He kept it tucked in his messenger bag everywhere he went, always prepared to chase a lead. Tonight, the bag sat slung over the back of his chair, the laptop balanced on his knees.

"Let's see if Lucien Grey actually exists," he murmured.

They searched local records first. Nothing. Then they widened the search to broader public databases, scanning for any mention of Lucien Grey in real estate transactions, obituaries, or business holdings. The results turned up scattered references but nothing that felt concrete. There was a Lucien Grey in London from decades ago, tied to an abandoned estate. Another mention of the name appeared in a genealogical site listing births from the 1890s. Each record was old, the location far away from present-day San Francisco. No current addresses popped up, no official presence.

"Strange," Ethan muttered, tapping the trackpad. "Without a birth date or a location, we can't confirm if it's the same person. He might just be a name repeated over different centuries, or it could be one man using an alias." His voice trailed off.

A chill crept along Ivy's spine. The wavering images of her childhood drawings floated in her memory. She'd scrawled the same face, the same name again and again, like an obsession that she didn't understand. She rubbed her arms, trying to ward off the cold sinking into her chest.

Ethan scrolled through digital archives. Some writings dated back to the early twentieth century, citing a mysterious figure rumored to be a spiritualist in Europe. Then in the 1950s, another rumor surfaced in old, unverified newspaper clippings about a Lucien Grey leading secret gatherings in North America. The language was half gossip, half cautionary tale.

"This is like chasing a ghost," Ethan said. "He doesn't stay in one place long, and none of these accounts prove he's the same person. Could be a family line or a string of impostors." He closed the laptop gently, letting out a tense breath. "But that doesn't explain why his name keeps following you."

Ivy could only shake her head, her gaze drifting to the vigil site across the street. The bright clusters of candles in Dolores Park still danced in the darkness. The quiet of that place clung to her, as though the dead man's final warning hovered in the air. She shivered.

Ethan reached for her hand again. The heat of his palm steadied her, reminding her that she was not alone in this. He angled his head, lowering his voice. "We will figure it out," he said. "Whoever Lucien Grey is, we'll find something eventually."

She wanted to believe that. She wanted to believe they could unravel this mystery with enough research and stubborn resolve. Yet a part of her knew the truth wove itself through deeper layers, through visions and half-forgotten childhood memories, through the glimpses of nightmares that sometimes felt too real. They finished their coffees in weighted silence, neither quite ready to lay out every fear on the table. When the waitress returned with the check, Ivy noticed the quiver in her own fingers. Her reflection in the cafe's tinted window revealed a woman who looked rattled, her eyes shadowed, her mouth pressed thin. She forced a small nod of thanks at the waitress, grateful for the warm interior even if it did little to calm her mind.

Outside, the cold air stung her cheeks. The vigil had thinned somewhat, people departing as the authorities stepped in. Ivy and Ethan walked in subdued quiet back to where he'd parked. Another ambulance cruised by, lights spinning. Ivy's lungs felt tight, as if the night's events pressed inward. She wanted to ask Ethan to stay with her, not for overt romance, but simply because the thought of being alone in her apartment felt too heavy to bear.

He seemed to sense her unspoken plea. Even as he unlocked the car, he gave her a measured look. "We can go to your place," he said quietly. "I'll stay long enough to make sure you're okay. Let you settle in. You shouldn't be alone."

Ivy exhaled an unsteady breath and nodded. She

noticed the tension in his posture, the soft look of concern in his eyes. He took it seriously, her rattled devotion to these visions and to the dead man's words. The city lights blurred past as they drove, neither of them speaking much, the hum of the engine filling the silence with a low vibration that mirrored the uneasy flutter in her gut.

When they reached her building, Ivy climbed out, wincing at the drizzle that had started to fall. They hurried upstairs to her apartment. Inside, she flipped on a single lamp, revealing the quiet warmth of her small living space. Books lay scattered across the coffee table, alongside a half-burned candle that had collected a pool of wax.

Ethan set his laptop on the couch. "You need anything?"

She shook her head. "I just need to breathe." She peeled off her coat and shoes, rubbing her arms as she moved to the kitchen for a glass of water. The normality of the routine calmed her somewhat. The water glinted in the yellowish overhead light when she took a sip.

Ethan waited, leaning against the arm of the couch, arms folded lightly. He looked ready to drop if she asked him to leave, but her chest tightened at the thought of him going. She walked over and sank onto the sofa. "Stay for a little while," she said, her voice stifled. "I'm not sure I can sleep after tonight."

His shoulders softened. He sat and reached tentatively for her hand. She let him hold it, allowing that connection to ease the knots in her stomach. For a long moment, they stayed like that, side by side on the couch, the lamp casting warm shadows around them. Outside, the drizzle grew into a faint tap against the windows.

Ivy felt exhaustion sweep through her like a current. She tried to fight it, but her eyes kept drooping shut. She was vaguely aware of Ethan standing, retrieving a blanket from a chair, and draping it over her shoulders. She mumbled a protest, but the weight of the night crushed her attempts at alertness.

"Get some rest," he said softly, his breath warm against her temple. She nodded, drifting in and out of a shallow doze. Though she did not fully remember him leaving, she thought she heard the soft click of the door eventually. Perhaps he lingered in the hallway a moment before disappearing into the misty night.

AT SOME INDETERMINATE POINT LATER, Ivy glimpsed herself standing in a desolate place. The dream formed around her like smoke. A glance revealed cracked pews, the overhead arches of an abandoned church. Moonlight, cold and silvery, filtered through broken stained-glass windows. Vines crept up the walls, twisted and thick, as if the building had been left to rot in some forgotten quarter of the city.

"Ivy," a voice called. It flowed from the shadows, low and eerie. She scanned the darkness between the stone columns. There, a figure stepped into a narrow shaft of moonlight. He wore a dark coat, slender and pristine, and his eyes gleamed as if they held mirrors. His face was painfully familiar, the same face she had once sketched so many times, the face she had convinced herself was a relic of her childhood nightmares.

She tried to speak, but her voice caught. A wave of cold dread spread through her. He moved closer, the silence stretching, until she could see the faint curve of his mouth as if he might smile.

I've been watching, he said softly. His voice threaded the air like silk, each word infused with quiet certainty. *You feel it, don't you?*

Ivy's heart pounded. She wanted to back away, but her body stayed rooted in place, as though compelled by some invisible force. In one wavering instant, she realized his presence in her visions had never gone away. He had always been there, shimmering in the corners of dream-scapes she refused to remember. Her lips parted, but no sound emerged.

He stepped forward again, close enough that she could see a faint luminous quality on his skin, something almost ageless. His gaze turned to her hands. *You found my name,* he said, an undercurrent of amusement in his tone. *And soon, you will need me.*

Despair threatened to crush her chest. She wanted to wake up, to tear herself free. She summoned all her will and pushed against the stagnant air of the church, struggling like someone pinned by an impossible weight.

The dream shattered.

Ivy jolted upright in her apartment, gasping for breath. Her nightshirt clung to her damp skin as if she had run a marathon. Moonlight probed through the window, revealing the empty living room. The blanket had slid off her shoulders. She placed a trembling hand over her heartbeat, trying to quiet the frantic rhythm. The echo of Lucien's words, *I've been watching*, pounded in her mind.

She pressed her back against the couch cushions, pulse racing, grappling with the renewed terror that he was not just some obscure name in a half-buried letter. He was real. His presence clung to her like a shadow, and her heart hammered as if trying to escape her ribs.

Outside, the rain tapped persistently, and the city slept on, unaware. Ivy swallowed a trembling breath, tears burning at the corners of her eyes. She could not stop the flood of dread that insisted Lucien was closer than ever before.

She stared at the faint reflection of her wide-eyed face in the dark window. For a moment, she thought she saw a second silhouette standing behind her. Then the image dissolved into the night. She was alone, heart pounding, with no answers and a new terror settling in her veins.

CHAPTER

TWO

THE MAN IN THE MIRROR

Ivy scrubbed her fingers across her cheeks, blinking at her reflection in the bathroom mirror. She felt unsteady on her feet, still rattled by the dream she had woken from minutes earlier. The small overhead light cast a pale-yellow glow across the sink and gave her face a wan look, as if she had just escaped a crisis. Her hair hung in disheveled curls around her shoulders, and she noticed a faint sheen of sweat on her temples. She stared at the mirror, bracing herself for something, or someone, to appear behind her.

A faint memory from her dream hovered at the edge of her thoughts. She had felt it earlier, the sensation of Lucien standing in a dimly lit church, calling her name in a quiet, haunting voice. Now her mind conjured his image in the bathroom reflection. She kept waiting for him to coalesce in the glass. But the tall, pale-eyed figure did not materialize. Instead, she caught movement behind her.

Robin stood in the doorway, toothbrush in hand, eyebrows knit with concern. She wore an oversized T-shirt and loose plaid pants, the picture of cozy domestic comfort. She studied Ivy with a gentle curiosity. "You look like you wrestled a ghost," she said, her voice muffled around the toothbrush bristles.

Ivy released a shaky breath and ran the water, splashing some on her face. "I think I did," she answered, though she offered no small laugh to lighten the mood. If anything, the corners of her eyes still burned with the echoes of the dream.

Robin spat in the sink and rinsed. She popped their toothbrush onto a small stand and grabbed a towel, offering it for Ivy to dry her hands. "I heard you muttering in your sleep. Something about an envelope, or I'm not actually sure. You sounded upset. Did you have another vision?"

She leaned her hips against the sink, letting the folded cotton of the towel rest in her hands. "Not quite a vision. More like a leftover haunting from last night. Actually, from everything these past few days." Her chest constricted as she remembered the vigil in *Dolores Park*, the hooded man's grasp on her wrist, that cryptic final whisper before he died at her feet. Then there was the second letter referencing Lucien Grey. "I dreamed of him again," Ivy murmured.

Robin nodded, her face serious. "Lucien." She exhaled quietly, as if the name itself carried weight. "You told me you've seen him in your dreams for years, but now he's actually showing up in real life?" Her shoulders tensed. "You never fully explained the letter. Or how you've been using your aunt's writings to track him. Maybe it's time you do."

Ivy lifted her gaze to meet Robin's. The reflection of the two of them in the mirror felt strangely intimate, her weary eyes, Robin's quiet determination. She pressed the towel to her palms. "I've tried not to dwell on him, or on the name," she said. "I was afraid that acknowledging his presence would open a door, one I wasn't ready to walk through."

"But you are ready now?"

She dropped her gaze from the mirror and padded out of the bathroom, nodding for Robin to follow her. The apartment's living area glowed with the faint morning light filtering through the window. Clouds dimmed the sky outside, and a layer of fog curled past the street, clinging to the building facades. She settled on the sofa, tucking her legs under her. After a brief hesitation, she patted the cushion beside her, inviting Robin to sit.

"I got an envelope back at the shop. Well, Ethan brought it to me." She paused, remembering the wave of dread she had felt seeing that wax seal. "It had Lucien's name in it, like a summons or a statement. Something about me beginning. About him waiting."

Robin's eyes glinted with worry. "Same kind of seal as before, right? The weird archaic design?"

Ivy nodded. "Yes, the same. And I have no idea who sent it, or why it showed up taped to my door. Ethan was worried. We looked for any obvious leads, but there's nothing. It's like Lucien Grey is a rumor whispered in the corners of old records. Or a name scribbled in half-rotted documents from a century ago."

Robin placed a comforting hand on her knee. "You must have recognized him from your childhood dreams. Is that how you pieced everything together?"

She inhaled, trying to steady the flutter in her stomach. "I realized just how many old sketches I had made. There's that sealed box at my parents' house, the drawings I did as a little girl. I would draw the same face over and over, labeling it L.G. I never even heard the name out loud back then, and yet I wrote it down like I had always known."

At the mention of those drawings, a chill danced across the back of her neck. She had returned to collect them only recently, rummaging under that loose floorboard in her old bedroom. All those charcoal sketches, all bearing the same signature: stern cheekbones, an amused tilt of the lips, and eyes that somehow felt older than anything else on the page. When she was six, it made no sense. Now it made too much sense, and that frightened her.

Robin frowned. "Does Ethan know you've had these dreams since childhood? That the drawings were so specific?"

Ivy pulled the blanket from the couch's arm over her lap. "He knows some of it. To be honest, I haven't told him the depth of it. It sounds too bizarre when I say it out loud. That I've dreamt of a man who might have lived, might still be alive, who might be something else entirely." Her throat felt tight. "But he's the same man referenced in the letter. The same man from last night's dream. The one the hooded stranger basically warned me about." She closed her eyes, hearing the milky-eyed man's final rasp echo in her memory. *You are not the first, and you are not the last.*

Robin's normally lively demeanor remained subdued as she considered Ivy's words. "What if this Lucien guy's real?" she asked softly. "Really out there, waiting, just like you fear. That's a big possibility, right?"

Ivy did not answer right away. In truth, her gut already told her the answer, that Lucien was not just some figment of imagination. She had felt it in her dreams, smelled the faint incense that lingered in every vision of him, and recognized the same presence in the edges of her mind when she was only half-awake. She swallowed, trying to push aside the wave of mounting anxiety.

"I know he's real," she said silently. "I just wish I knew what he claims to want." She gave Robin a wavering smile. "And if he's dangerous, or if I'm just paranoid."

Robin squeezed her shoulder, her eyes gleaming with an unspoken vow of support. "Let's look at Cassandra's journals again," she suggested. "You told me she's written about Lucien, or at least about a man with those same eyes. We have the stack of volumes she gave you after you confronted her, right? Maybe there's a clue hidden somewhere."

Ivy nodded, already rising from the couch. "I keep them in that trunk." She pointed to a worn, wooden chest near a tall bookshelf. She had arranged them in neat stacks after the fiasco with the man at the vigil, searching for any mention of cryptic phrases that might tie back to the envelope. She had found references to a shadowy figure who drifted through the circles of old seers, but nothing concrete on what he planned or how he fit into the tapestry of her nightmares.

Together, they knelt next to the trunk. Robin lifted the lid, allowing the faint scent of old parchment and dried herbs to seep into the room. Cassandra had stored sprigs of lavender and rosemary amidst the journals, presumably to preserve them. Ivy began rifling through the carefully stacked spines, scanning the inscriptions for any sign of L.G.

Robin angled a small lamp for better reading light. She hummed with each turn of the brittle pages. "Some of this is messy scrawl in your aunt's handwriting. And some are your grandmother's, right?"

Ivy nodded. "Yes. I guess they were all trying to document something beyond normal comprehension."

She paused, flipping slowly through a thick tome bound in dark leather. The stream of old ink on the page resembled shapes that might be eyes or swirling constellations. "I vaguely remember Cassandra showing me this last time I visited. She said something about how some lines might vanish if you do not understand them, or how certain passages need to be read under candlelight. Some seer trick, I guess."

"Then let's see if we can glean anything. If last night's dream was so strong, maybe the right page will stand out." Robin held the lamp closer.

Ivy continued turning pages, searching for anything referencing the name Lucien. At times, she paused at half-legible lines describing rituals or warnings like *The line between watchers and devourers is thin*, or *He reemerges when the world forgets*. None explicitly stated L.G., yet the vibe left her uneasy. The lamp's light caught a faint type-written page pressed between older sheets. This was unusual, given that the rest was handwritten. Curious, Ivy slipped that page out.

Robin raised an eyebrow. "Anything?"

"It's blank," she said quietly, puzzling over the single piece of yellowed paper. The lamp's glow revealed faint outlines, as though old words had been erased. She placed it aside and kept going. More pages fluttered under her fingertips until she reached the final third of the journal. There, a small illustration caught her eye. Someone had drawn a face in startling detail: a man with sharp cheek-bones, an angled jaw, and an almost playful curve to the mouth. The caption beneath it read, *L.G.* She stared, trans-fixed by the resemblance to the face she had sketched as a child.

Robin leaned closer, her mouth parted slightly. "That is definitely the same man you drew," she murmured. "Same expression, same shape of the nose."

Ivy inhaled slowly. The drawing was labeled in a cursive script that looked older than Cassandra's hand-writing, possibly from her late grandmother's notes. A short line followed the initials.

The dream traveler with pale eyes and a cunning grin.

She felt a tremor pass through her chest. She pressed her palm against the page, feeling the uneven ridges of the pencil marks. Suddenly, she remembered the night in Dolores Park, that cryptic final message.

To Lucien Grey—she has begun.

It connected to everything about L.G. She found it impossible to ignore the tie. He had to be real. Or at least, real enough to disturb the entire lineage of seers in her family.

Her mind churned. "He was real in these journals, too," she whispered. "A figure recognized by more than one generation. I just wish the text said more. It doesn't say how to stop him, or even how to talk to him." She let out a shaky laugh. "Not that I want to talk to him, exactly. But you know what I mean."

Robin grimaced. "I do. Knowledge is power, right? Maybe Cassandra knows more than she has let on."

"I talked to her about him briefly once, and she got silent, as if she was trying to keep me from prying." Ivy closed the journal, hugging it to her chest. "If my aunt believes Lucien is a threat, I want to figure out why." She glanced around the apartment, uneasy. "I'm worried that me seeing him in my dreams means something bigger is happening."

Robin set aside the lamp, resting a comforting hand on Ivy's shoulder. "We can go through more journals. Or we can call Cassandra. We can face that conversation whether or not she likes it."

A curious queasiness twisted in Ivy's stomach at the thought of confronting her aunt again. Recent discussions with Cassandra had been tense. Their strained relationship made these revelations come in fragments, and it might take prodding to get a straight answer. Still, drifting along in the dark felt worse.

She straightened, taking a few slow breaths. "We can try calling her this afternoon," she offered. "If she avoids me, I will keep digging for clues on my own."

Robin nodded in agreement, then tapped the cover of the journal. "So, you have a name, a face, and a documented note that your grandmother encountered him. That suggests he is more than a rumor. If you dreamed of him, and he's relevant to the letter you got, we need to be careful."

Ivy's fingers tightened on the worn leather. "He might be connected to the entire reason that hooded man approached me in Dolores Park. Or maybe Lucien orchestrated that vigil. I can't tell." She swallowed, meeting Robin's gaze. "I only know something is happening beneath the surface. If Lucien Grey is alive, and if he's watching me, I need to be ready."

Robin gripped her hand. "Then we'll be ready together, yeah?"

A hint of gratitude warmed Ivy's chest. "Thank you," she whispered. She squeezed back, feeling a fragile sense of camaraderie during all that confusion. Outside, the fog clung to the glass like a curtain. She envisioned Lucien out there somewhere, standing in dim light, perhaps waiting to make a pivot onto center stage. The thought both chilled and fascinated her.

They rose and brought the journal to the coffee table. Ivy's pulse hammered, thinking about the oracles, illusions, and cryptic references. She refused to be helpless. As she reached for a notepad on the table, she realized her phone was buzzing from the kitchen counter. She held up a hand, quietly stepping away to check the caller ID. Her breath caught when she saw Ethan's name. A complicated sweep of relief and apprehension coursed through her, and she debated letting it go to voicemail. She cared for him deeply, but she also wondered how to explain her intensifying sense of dread.

After a moment's hesitation, she picked up. "Hey," she said softly, pressing the phone to her ear.

"Hi," Ethan answered in that subdued, cautious tone he got whenever he presumed she might be upset. "I just wanted to see how you're holding up after last night. I know you barely slept. Did you get any rest?"

Ivy glanced over at Robin, who sat flipping through more pages of Cassandra's journals. "Not really," she admitted. "Too many nightmares." She forced a small smile, though he could not see it. "I'm going to keep investigating everything I can about him."

Ethan's breath sounded heavier. "Yeah. I've been doing my own digging, but I keep hitting dead ends. It's like Lucien Grey vanished off the face of the earth, or never existed in the first place. But I see your drawings, I see these references in that second envelope. I can't ignore that someone is actively pointing me, or you, toward him."

She heard the concern shading Ethan's words. It reassured her a bit, knowing he took the warnings seriously. Still, she felt a pang of guilt that she had not told him about the deeper connection she shared with Lucien, the strange feeling that their paths had crossed before she was even old enough to comprehend it. She steeled herself to be more forthcoming soon.

"I'll keep you posted," she murmured. "Right now, I have Robin helping me sort through old journals. Maybe we can compare notes later?"

"Sounds good. I'll talk to you soon." He paused, the silence crackling over the line. "Stay safe, Ivy."

She swallowed and ended the call gently. Warmth spilled through her chest at his parting words, but it was short-lived. As she set the phone down, she returned to the couch, resuming her careful search. Page by page, Robin and Ivy found passing references to a traveling seer, an unusual figure who came and went through hidden circles. The next mention of L.G. was scribbled in the margin of an unfinished entry: *He stands at the crossroads. He arms new seers with illusions.* Then the writing trailed off into blotchy ink stains.

Ivy felt her heart twist. "So if this is Lucien, he's not here as a passive observer. He arms new seers with illusions. Maybe that means he influences their visions. Or manipulates them to deepen their power. That might explain why I'm seeing him more often."

Robin rubbed the back of their neck. "Which also implies he's fed clarifying illusions to you, right? If you keep dreaming of him, maybe that dream is something he actively wants you to see."

She shut the journal and let out a breath. "I hate the idea of someone else meddling with my mind. But you might be right." They fell quiet, letting the revelation settle, thick as the fog outside.

The silence broke when Robin exhaled shakily. "I'm sorry if this is overwhelming. I wish I had better advice."

Ivy slipped the journal onto the table and covered Robin's hand with her own. "You're doing plenty by being here. Really," she said, her voice stifled. In the next moment, her gaze landed on that older sketch again. The man's faintly amused mouth seemed to mock her. "He was real," she said, thinking of the letter, the notebooks, her earliest memories, "and dangerous."

They decided they could not let fear drive the rest of the evening. Robin suggested a break, and soon Ethan arrived with takeout from the corner Thai place. The three of them gathered on the floor around Ivy's coffee table, trading jokes while spicy aromas filled the apartment. For a precious hour they allowed themselves to laugh about old memories, to share inside jokes about customers at the shop, to breathe without looking over their shoulders.

Ivy felt the fragile comfort of a family she had chosen, not one bound by blood or the treacherous threads of fate. Ethan leaned back against the couch, smiling in that tired way of his, while Robin commandeered the television remote to queue up a ridiculous comedy. As the opening credits rolled, Ivy nestled between them, their shoulders touching, and for the first time in days her pulse slowed. She knew the world outside still churned with shadows, but here was a brief sanctuary, a reminder that whatever waited ahead, she wouldn't face it alone.

THREE

VISITORS AND VERSIONS

Ivy stood on the sidewalk outside Cassandra's tall townhouse, clutching her jacket against the cool evening air. A line of ivy curled around the front gate, its glossy leaves shining in the faint glow of the old-fashioned lamp overhead. She could smell the faint tang of city fog drifting in from the bay. Nervous energy pooled inside her, the same quiver she felt whenever she crossed the threshold into her aunt's domain. Strange that she could read for clients without blinking, yet a meeting with Cassandra always twisted her stomach in knots.

She raised her hand to knock, but the door opened before her knuckles touched the wood. Cassandra stood in the entryway, draped in a flowing sweater of smoky gray. The hallway lamp gave her an almost ethereal silhouette, emphasizing the silver at her temples. She offered Ivy a faint, inscrutable smile.

"Come in," Cassandra said. "Our visitor is waiting."

Ivy exhaled, stepping into the corridor. Candlelight in

stained-glass sconces lit the hallway, their colors splashing shards of green and violet across the floor. Faint flute music played from the next room, forlorn and tremulous. The house smelled of old books, lavender, and some incense Ivy couldn't name. She closed the door quietly behind her, feeling its weight thud against the frame.

"How did you even meet this visitor?" Ivy asked in a low voice, falling into step behind her aunt. "You only said she's from the old Circle."

Cassandra's shoulders tensed. "It is more accurate to say the Circle that once was. Thalia claims there are remnants, people who never abandoned the cause after the betrayal. She asked for you by name."

Ivy felt her heartbeat kick up a notch. She tried to keep her voice even. "She asked specifically for me?"

"She did," Cassandra said, glancing back with an expression equal parts concern and curiosity. "When I mentioned you, her excitement bordered on awe. She made sure you would be here this evening."

A chill grazed Ivy's skin, as though an invisible hand ran a fingertip down her arm. The echo of her childhood dreams lingered in her mind, half-visible shapes that once haunted her sketches. She pressed her lips together, silently following Cassandra to the sitting room.

They entered a warm space illuminated by a single lamp on the side table. Shelves lined the walls, stuffed with old tomes whose leather spines had begun to crack. Aromatic candles glowed on the mantle beneath a framed mirror that was covered in pale linen. A tall woman with dark braided hair stood there, inspecting the candle flames. She wore a long tunic of muted gold and had a set of wooden beads looped around her wrists. When she turned, Ivy first noticed her fathomless eyes, deep with something that felt older than memory.

"You must be Ivy," the woman said softly. Her voice held a gentleness that invited calm, but there was unmistakable strength beneath it. "I am Thalia."

Ivy paused, uncertain how to greet her. "Yes," she managed, clearing her throat. "I've just arrived."

Thalia stepped forward and, without warning, gently brushed Ivy's hair back from her face. The gesture was intimate, more so than a typical handshake or polite hello. "You favor your grandmother," she murmured, letting her fingers linger near Ivy's temple. "I see the same shape of the eyes, the same quiet determination in your bones."

Something about Thalia's confidence made Ivy's nerves flutter. The woman's closeness felt oddly reassuring, though Ivy's mind clamored with questions. Thalia was a stranger, but she carried herself as if she had known Ivy for years. Cassandra motioned toward a small cluster of seats around a low table and invited them both to sit.

Ivy sank into one of the armchairs, glancing in mild confusion as Thalia settled across from her. Cassandra went to retrieve the teapot from a sideboard. The melodic notes of the flute music continued, distant and unobtrusive, giving the sitting room an otherworldly air. Ivy laced her fingers together just to keep them still. There was a moment's quiet until Cassandra returned, placing a silver tray on the table. Steam drifted lazily from the pot's spout. She offered a tiny, graceful nod to Thalia, then served each of them. Ivy felt the eyes of both women on her as she raised the cup to her lips. The calm taste of chamomile and lemongrass spread across her tongue.

Cassandra sat last, folding her hands neatly in her lap. "So, Thalia, you said you come bearing news of the Circle?"

Thalia inclined her head. "Yes, though news might be too small a word. The Circle once spanned entire coasts, gathering gifted souls to anchor the intangible currents that the rest of the world ignores. Much of that has fallen apart in recent decades. Betrayals, illusions, and the tragedy we all know too well." She paused, glancing at Ivy.

"But some of us have tried to preserve the older ways. Others want to create new ways. All of us are watching for signals, for a spark."

Ivy felt her cheeks warm. She set her cup down, determined to keep her composure. "Why would they watch for me? I'm barely in control of my own visions, and sometimes I wonder if they even help at all."

"It is not about control," Thalia said gently. "It is about possibility. You have a capacity. The question is whether you will bury it, or whether you will learn to bear it."

Ivy bristled, her pride lighting up like a match tip. "Sounds a bit cultish," she muttered, forcing a small, dry laugh. "I've never considered myself part of an organization, old or new."

Thalia took a careful sip of her tea before continuing. "You have no reason to trust me. In fact, few would blame you for refusing any open hand after what you have experienced. But I must tell you this. The remnants of the old

Circle are not seeking to recruit blindly. We are seeking to safeguard those with certain gifts. We cannot afford to lose more individuals like your grandmother."

Ivy's throat constricted. She directed a look at Cassandra, who stared at Thalia in measured silence. "What do you know of my grandmother, exactly?" Ivy asked. Her tone was quiet, weighed down by complicated memories of old journals and half-spoken family secrets.

"That she had a power akin to weaving," Thalia said. "She shaped glimpses of the future into something that might be changed, if one was bold enough to try. She taught many of us, though I studied from afar, traveling between enclaves. I encountered her once, near the end, when she stood at the crossroads of a choice that might have saved the Circle from falling. But the price was too high."

Cassandra stiffened, her eyes darkening with an old, buried sorrow. Ivy drummed her fingers on the armrest, resisting the urge to demand details about that fateful choice. The name of her grandmother always unlocked conflicting emotions, fascination, heartbreak, longing. She inhaled, trying to keep her voice steady.

"But why mention her now?"

Thalia held Ivy's gaze. "Because you carry on where she left off. There is a reason you see more clearly than others. You were meant to continue a legacy, not just survive it. We have observed your visions, your caution, the times you touched the edges of truths others fear. These are not accidents."

A silence fell. Cassandra's expression was unreadable,

though her lips parted slightly, as if she wanted to speak but chose not to interrupt. Ivy grappled with a flare of unease. She couldn't decide if those words made her feel flattered, frightened, or both.

"I never asked to inherit anything," Ivy said at last, her voice subdued.

Thalia leaned forward, resting her palms on her knees. "No one truly asks. Yet you have it, and you have begun to awaken it. The old Circle recognized how certain bloodlines resonate with the deeper currents. Some families produce dreamers, others produce guardians. Your line produces those who see beyond the first horizon." She paused, then gave a slight smile. "I only speak plainly because you deserve honesty. We do not want to trap you. We want to acknowledge you."

Ivy tried to gather her thoughts, but everything spun in a rush of emotions. Her mind returned to the cryptic letter she once received about someone named Lucien Grey, the quiet illusions in the corners of her dreams that had recently become sharper. She recalled how her sketches from childhood matched real faces she met years later. Maybe Thalia had a point. It was never random.

She released a shaky breath. "It still sounds cult-like, no matter how kindly you phrase it. I appreciate the honesty, but is the old Circle honestly any different from a cult with fancy rituals?"

Thalia's smile grew wry. "True cults demand subservience. They blind you with dogma. The Circle, at its best, was an alliance of seers who supported each other's gifts while shaping visions for the good of the many. At its worst, it was undone by greed. You stand at a juncture where you might shape a new path or let the old cycle repeat. I suspect your vantage is far richer than you realize."

Ivy could feel Cassandra's gaze overhead like a watchful hawk. The mention of shaping a new path sent a strange ripple through her chest, a sense that she was standing on a razor's edge, uncertain and alive. She thought of her recent nightmares. She thought of the hooded man who had died with cryptic words on his lips. If Thalia had been a part of that hidden network for so long, maybe she had more answers than Ivy could glean from a handful of aged journals.

"How many remain in your group?" Cassandra asked quietly, taking the role of skeptic.

"Not many," Thalia admitted. "A few in different states, some across the Atlantic. We are scattered. Some call themselves by new names, trying to hide from the memory of what happened before. Yet a few remain dedicated to the idea that we can unify again, especially if we, but that is not for me to press on you now."

A short silence followed. The candles on the mantle wavered, sending shapeshifting shadows across the carpet. Ivy's lips parted, though no immediate words emerged. It unsettled her that Thalia knew so much without having set foot in Ivy's life before tonight. At the same time, it tugged at the lonely corners of Ivy's heart, the corners that yearned for community.

Thalia shifted in her seat, pulling a small pouch from the folds of her tunic. She placed it on the table between them with deliberate care. "An offering," she said simply. "Dried herbs, pressed leaves. They come from a time when your grandmother guided one of our gatherings. I think they might show you glimpses of how she worked, if you choose to use them. Or you can throw them away. It is your choice."

Cassandra eyed the pouch warily. Ivy swallowed. She reached out and picked it up, feeling its soft cloth and the faint rustle of something fragile inside. The mention of glimpses made her pulse flutter. She was not entirely sure she wanted to see more, yet her curiosity prodded her to accept.

"Why now?" Ivy asked, setting the pouch gently in her lap. "I've been having visions for a while. Why reveal yourself all of a sudden?"

"Because your aura flares brighter than ever," Thalia said, her tone warm and urgent. "You have already stirred energies some of us thought dormant. The movement has begun, and so has the danger. In carefully placed corners of the city, people talk of a seer who stands at the threshold, perhaps repeating tragedies or forging new outcomes. You must decide which it will be. I came to warn you that the Circle still breathes. Parts of it want you to join. Others might see you as a threat."

Ivy's mind spun. She caught Cassandra's expression, a mixture of distant regret and quiet resolve. Her aunt had never been one to volunteer details about the old ways, yet she too had once been a formidable seer, someone who had pulled away after some disaster Ivy still knew too little about. In the silence, Ivy thought she heard the faint clinking of the wooden beads around Thalia's wrists. The stillness pressed on her lungs.

Finally, Ivy found her voice. "Danger." She exhaled, tasting the word. "Like what?"

Thalia gave a slow shake of her head. "All gifts come with costs. If you break illusions, you can expose those who profit from them. If you weave illusions, you might trap yourself in your own web. The old Circle had painful lessons on both counts. It is not a trifling matter."

Ivy bit back a reply about how she never asked to be the focal point of anything. She felt Cassandra's hand touch her shoulder gently, as if steadying her. The room was so quiet that Ivy noticed the rhythmic patter of her own heartbeat. She realized, in that moment, she did not want to be ignorant anymore. She wanted to know precisely what she risked.

Thalia eased back in her chair and finished the last sip of her tea. She set down the cup with a soft click against the saucer. The colorful glow of the stained-glass sconces danced on her face. Ivy's mouth went dry. She laced and unlaced her fingers, certain that Thalia had more to say, more warnings, more insight about the old Circle's splintered remains. Ivy had spent so long grappling with her visions alone. The possibility of a greater network, broken though it might be, stirred a spark of longing in her chest. If Thalia spoke truly, Ivy might gain perspective on the twisting path of destiny that haunted her dreams.

She settled her gaze on Thalia. "You talk like I'm already in a cult," she said, forcing a small, sardonic smile, "but you also sound like you're trying to help."

She felt Cassandra's presence at her side, and her aunt's tension seemed to ease just a fraction. The single sentence hung in the air, carrying the weight of Ivy's curiosity, her fear, and her blossoming need for answers. Whatever Thalia would say next might upend her world further, but Ivy was done living half-blind to everything going on around her.

She leaned forward, heart pounding. "Tell me more."

Thalia exchanged a look with Cassandra before speaking again. "The Circle began as a gathering of idealists," she explained, "seers who believed they could map out the most dangerous futures and steer society away from them. Decades ago we attempted a weaving that would stitch multiple visions together." She paused, the memory pulsing in her eyes. "Something went wrong. A surge of power lashed back. Several of our members were caught inside the illusion and never woke."

Cassandra nodded, her expression grim. "We lost good people, including a close friend of your grandmother's. In the aftermath, some of us blamed the technique, others blamed ambition. The Circle fractured. That accident," Thalia continued quietly, "is why many fear seeing the Circle rise again. The power we channeled nearly tore a hole in the city. Those who survived scattered and swore never to weave on that scale again."

Ivy listened, stunned. The vague references she had heard in passing suddenly took shape. The cost of misusing visions wasn't just personal. It could break minds and lives. No wonder Cassandra flinched whenever Ivy mentioned joining.

"So when we worry about you getting involved," Cassandra said gently, "understand that it isn't about doubting your potential. It's about remembering how easily the Circle's purpose can twist when someone pushes too far."

FOUR

AN INVITATION WRITTEN IN SMOKE

Ivy stood at the narrow counter in her apartment's small kitchen, ladle held aloft, focusing intently on the simmering sauce in front of her. The stove's yellowish overhead light lent everything a blur of warmth, and she found that comforting as she stirred. She could see Ethan's reflection in the glass of the cabinet doors. He was chopping vegetables with the type of meticulous focus he usually reserved for his investigations. The rhythmic crack of the knife punctuated their soft conversation, a familiar domestic sound that managed to calm her nerves.

She let out a breath, trying to center herself. The faint smell of garlic and rosemary coiled upward in the steam. Some part of her clung to the simple normalcy of cooking dinner with the man she cared about. Their life had never been peaceful, not since the moment she first realized she might be more than an ordinary tarot reader, but any fleeting stillness felt like a gift.

"You sure you want the peppers in slices?" Ethan

asked, turning slightly to look at her. Tension edged his voice, even if the question itself was mundane.

Ivy nodded. "Thin slices," she said, stirring the ladle once more in the pot. "They cook faster that way." She tasted the sauce with a quick sip from a wooden spoon. Tangy heat spread across her tongue, and she decided it needed more salt.

Ethan set his knife down and reached for the salt-shaker on the counter. "Here."

She offered a thankful smile and sprinkled more salt into the sauce. They had developed this fluid rhythm in the kitchen recently. He had insisted that cooking together might be good for them. "Team-building," he had joked after one of their many misunderstandings, and she had reluctantly agreed to give it a try. Now, the easy pattern of stirring and chopping was one of the few times she didn't feel the weight of her gift pressing in.

From the living room, Robin's laughter bubbled. She was sprawled across Ivy's old couch, scrolling on their phone and humming tunelessly under their breath. Occasionally, she teased Ivy and Ethan about looking like a married couple preparing a holiday feast, which always made Ethan grin crookedly. Ivy would respond with an eye roll, but she secretly savored that sense of ordinary closeness, something she wasn't sure she'd ever felt while growing up in an anxious household.

She turned off the burner and peeked at Ethan's progress. He was wiping peppers off the cutting board into a pan. There was a strain behind his eyes, though. Exhaustion, or apprehension, or both. She recognized it because it lived inside her, too, ever since the city seemed to tilt sideways with the endless stream of letters, cryptic visions, and revelations about the old Seer's Circle. Even mild chores felt heavy when the rest of the world was so uncertain.

A sudden shuffle at the front door made her freeze. The stirring spoon clattered against the pot's rim, droplets of sauce splattering across her knuckles. She winced, stepping back from the stove. Ethan's head snapped up.

"Did you hear that?" he asked, tension sharpening his tone.

Robin sat straighter on the couch. "Someone slipped something under the door."

Ivy wiped her hands on a dish towel and moved into the living room. The overhead light fixture buzzed softly, casting shadows across the floor. She crouched near the door and found a pristine white envelope lying on the welcome mat. It was large, as though containing something rigid. She picked it up carefully. Her heart hammered. Her fingers already recognized the subtle chill of an unexpected message.

She stared at the envelope. No writing on the front or back, no return address, no postage. Just her name, Ivy, scrawled in a delicate script. The scrawl looked almost familiar, though she couldn't place it exactly. It took her a moment to realize her hand was trembling. A faint voice inside her mind whispered that she might not want to open it here, with Ethan and Robin watching. But she had learned not to hide every secret from them. Or so she tried to convince herself.

She glanced back at Ethan. He had come alongside her, wiping his damp hands on a stray dish towel. "Another one of those?" he asked. His concern was buried under frustration. She couldn't blame him. Notes, letters, and cryptic envelopes seemed to mark her days now.

Robin muttered, "One day, maybe someone will just knock before leaving all these creepy messages."

Ivy inhaled, then slipped a fingernail beneath the sealed flap and tore it open. Inside was a single card with gold-inked lettering that glimmered under the overhead light. One word jumped off the page.

Sanctuary.

Beneath it lay an address, also in metallic gold print. No date, no instructions, nothing else. Just that one word and a place somewhere in the city that Ivy didn't recognize, though it looked like it might be in Chinatown. She traced a fingertip across the embossed letters, feeling an inexplicable flutter in her chest.

Ethan leaned over her shoulder, close enough that she felt his breath skim her ear. "Sanctuary," he read aloud. "This city is running out of synonyms for secret hideouts?"

She tried to steady her pulse. "We've heard that word before. Some people refer to the old Seer's Circle base as a sanctuary. But I didn't think it was the official name."

Robin brushed a stray tuft of dyed hair from her forehead. "Could be just a fancy name for another ritual site. Or maybe it's a new front for shady business. Are we not over the cryptic addresses yet?"

Ethan pressed his lips thin. "If it's from whoever's behind these manipulations, it feels like bait." His voice was low, almost a growl. "I don't like it."

Ivy nodded, though her curiosity stirred. She felt pulled, as if the single word on the card carried a subtle gravitational force. She couldn't help recalling how she had encountered Lucien, and how terrifying and intriguing that had felt. The city and the illusions within it rarely gave her direct answers. Yet here was a tangible address. A place that might tell her something she didn't already know. She wanted to see it.

"I can't just ignore it," she said quietly. "We keep waiting for pieces of the puzzle to surface. Maybe we should see what they're offering."

Ethan's jaw tightened. "See what they're offering, or walk right into a trap?" He reached for the card, but Ivy slipped it behind her back, stepping out of his immediate reach. The tension that flared between them caught her off guard, though she suspected it had been building for days.

She forced a careful tone. "We can't hide forever. We know that these behind-the-scenes figures have been nudging me or watching me." Her voice fell. "I need to know what's going on."

Robin cleared her throat. "But do you have to go? Like, do you have to see it in person? We can call someone. Or do some pre-scouting." They paused. "You know. Something safer."

Ivy shut her eyes for a moment, feeling a maze of conflicting energies. She replayed the many times she had let a letter or an omen push her to take caution. She remembered how even caution had not prevented that hooded stranger at the vigil from grabbing her. And she remembered how she still ended up with more questions than answers. She was tired of living in partial dark, waiting for her next vision to unravel the knot.

She opened her eyes. "No. I need to check it out. I can't keep letting these letters or these illusions control my every move. Whoever, or whatever, is behind this, I want to see it on my terms."

Her determination only made Ethan's gaze frost over. He ran a hand through his hair. "Let me come with you," he said. She heard the rawness under his words. "If it's truly a trap, you might need backup."

She considered him, the man she trusted enough to stand beside her through every bizarre revelation. But something in her gut said that if Sanctuary was linked to deeper corners of the seer world, then taking Ethan might complicate everything. He was deeply loyal but also deeply skeptical, and that had caused friction whenever they encountered pure mystical phenomena. She worried about him stepping into a place that might warp hostages, illusions, or entire rooms of unsuspecting minds. She also worried about the effect her powers could have, especially if she was a conduit. Perhaps it would be safer if she braved it alone. At least this once.

She glanced down at the card, golden letters shining in the overhead light. "I think I should go by myself."

Ethan flinched, as if she'd slapped him. "You're seriously letting me get sidelined on this? The last time you ran off alone..."

She held up a hand before he could finish. "I know," she said, her voice trembling just a bit. "I remember. But this time, I'll be careful." She lowered her hand. "I need to show them that I'm not cowering. I need to make a stand, even if it's small."

Ethan's eyes flashed. "So that's it. You've decided."

She took a breath, forcing the kitchen's warm scents and the glow of the single overhead bulb to ground her. "Yes," she said. "I've decided. It might not be the best choice, but if I don't go, I'll never know."

Robin cut in with a hesitant laugh. "If you're the fish, you're at least the type that can sprout piranha teeth when you're cornered."

Ivy appreciated the levity, but she still felt Ethan's disapproval radiate through the room like a pulse. She turned to face him fully, card in hand. "I'm leaving tomorrow," she said. "I'll find out what or who is waiting for me there, gather information, and come back. I'm not walking into anything reckless. I promise."

Ethan shook his head. The tension in his shoulders bunched tight. "Ivy, this is reckless by definition. You're letting them control the narrative. Don't you see that?"

Ivy swallowed and set the envelope on the coffee table, letting the card rest on top. "I see that if I don't do something, I'll live with the uncertainty." Her voice shook slightly. "And right now, I'm done letting these shadows dictate my life from the corners. If they want me at this Sanctuary, then I'll see it for myself."

He exhaled slowly, setting both hands on his hips, as though trying not to argue further in Robin's presence. "Fine," he said at last. "But I will be two blocks away. I am not leaving you to walk in there with no backup at all."

She started to protest, but he held up a finger. "That's not negotiable, Ivy. You can't stop me from going somewhere near that address. I'm not letting you vanish, no matter what."

Her heart softened. She wanted to push further, insist on complete solitude, but she also knew that Ethan rarely budged once he set a boundary. She nodded, feeling relief even in the midst of the argument. "All right," she said quietly. "We'll work out the details tomorrow." She managed a faint, weary smile. "For now, can we try to finish dinner?"

He let out a bitter scoff. "I've lost my appetite," he admitted, scrubbing a hand over his face. "I'm sorry." He shot Robin a pained look, then glanced at Ivy again. "I just need to clear my head."

For a moment, the three of them stood silent, the overhead lamp blinking. Ivy pressed her lips together, unsure how to ease the tension in him. She stepped closer, but Ethan shook his head faintly, turning toward the door. She felt the sting of rejection pierce her chest.

Robin stayed perched on the couch, fiddling with the edge of a pillow. Her eyes darted between Ivy and Ethan, evidently unsure whether to intervene.

Ethan tossed the dish towel aside, grabbed his jacket from the hook, and slammed it on. "If you change your mind about going alone," he said, meeting Ivy's gaze firmly, "call me." Then he stepped to the front door. "Please," he added, his voice gentler.

Ivy didn't move, even as a rush of guilt washed through her. "I will," she forced out. She saw him hesitate, but then he pulled open the door, letting the hallway's dim light spill in. A second later, the door shut behind him, leaving her to realize she hadn't convinced him of anything. She was still determined to do what needed to be done.

Robin cleared her throat. "Want me to put these peppers away?" Her attempt at casualness made Ivy smile gratefully.

"Sure," she answered softly. "Might as well. I doubt either of us can pick up where we left off tonight."

Robin padded over to the kitchen counter and busied herself with storing the vegetables in a container. Ivy lingered near the living room window, peering outside. Fog pressed against the glass, the street below a blur of orange lamplight. A part of her wanted to run out, chase Ethan, apologize for everything she couldn't explain. But she also knew that a deeper part of her wouldn't abandon what she felt compelled to discover.

In the quiet, Robin stacked plates in the sink. Then she hopped up onto the kitchen counter and folded her arms across their chest. "So," Robin prompted. "Tomorrow. Sanctuary. You actually going through with this?"

Ivy nodded, stepping to the coffee table. She picked up the gold-lettered card, feeling its edges dig lightly into her fingertips. "I am. And I really do feel like I can't ignore it." She exhaled, setting it back down. "I'm not seeking out another confrontation. But something is calling me." She shook her head. "Saying that out loud sounds ridiculous."

"Not ridiculous. Just real." Robin tapped the countertop. "You do realize Ethan wants to protect you from all that. But you're not just this delicate flower he needs to lock away in a greenhouse." A hint of amusement curled their lips. "You're a stubborn rose with suspicious thorns, or a shark with anxiety. Take your pick."

Ivy huffed a small laugh.

Robin wagged a finger. "I get it. You've had your fill of reactive living. You want to be proactive. Just promise me you'll stay aware of any weird vibes the moment you step into that address. If it feels off, you get out."

Ivy set the card in her purse, methodically sliding it into an inner pocket. "I swear. I won't do anything reckless. I only want to see what they want from me. If it's dangerous, I'll leave."

Robin relaxed slightly. "All right. Because we both know some people in these circles can be good, but some can be, well, let's just say they have agendas."

Ivy nodded, thinking of Lucien, thinking of the hooded man in Dolores Park, thinking of all the quiet hints that bigger forces were at play. "I won't forget."

A silence settled. The apartment seemed strangely still, lacking Ethan's steady presence. Ivy sank onto the couch. Her gaze roamed over the living room, scattered candles, half-read journals stacked near the lamp, and the faint burn mark on the wooden floor from an earlier mishap with incense. She had thrown herself into so many unknowns already. Yet she kept surviving, kept finding new layers of truth. Maybe going to this address was the next step. Maybe it was the final step toward realizing what she really was.

"You look lost in your thoughts," Robin said softly, hopping off the counter and moving closer to the couch. "Wanna talk about it?"

She patted the seat beside her, and Robin settled next to her. A faint tinge of garlic and pepper still lingered in the air. "I'm tired of feeling like I'm behind. Like I'm a puppet who never sees who's pulling the strings," she murmured. "This could be the moment I cut those strings."

Robin nodded thoughtfully. "And Ethan?"

Ivy's chest tightened. "He just wants me safe," she said. "But safety is subjective now, isn't it? Do I hide forever, or do I step out and face what I've been running from?"

They bumped her shoulder gently. "You know he'll come around. He just hates the idea of you getting hurt."

"I know," Ivy agreed. "I hate it, too." Her throat felt tight. "But I need to do this."

Robin gave a firm nod. "Then you do it."

Ivy looked at the clock on the wall. The sauce on the stove had stopped steaming, the soft hiss gone silent. Tomorrow morning, she would follow that address and see what Sanctuary meant. And if it changed everything again, well, at least she'd be facing it on her own terms. She pressed her hand over the purse where the card lay.

FIVE

ENTER LUCIEN GREY

Ivy gathered her courage at the threshold of the narrow Chinatown bookstore. Neon signs glowed overhead, creating washes of orange and pink that danced across the old brick. She studied the store's unremarkable sign, its paint faded, Chinese characters partially obscured by layers of grime. From the outside, it looked like any tucked-away shop offering tea sets or medicinal herbs. She could smell sweet incense mingling with the scent of garlic from a nearby restaurant. The city around her hummed with life, clanging pots, chattering voices, the rattle of a late-night bus. Yet she felt separate from it all, balanced on a precipice between sense and illusion.

She worked the tension from her fingers. Her purse, slung close, carried the gold-inked card that had beckoned her here. The single word, Sanctuary, had seared itself into her mind from the moment it arrived under her apartment door. Alone. She was alone this evening because she had insisted that she did not need Ethan hovering in the shadows. She told herself it was safer for him. Whether that was the truth or a protective lie, she could not say. Her heart still twisted at the thought of the argument they had left unresolved.

"Get it done," she whispered under her breath, as if willing herself not to turn and walk away. She checked the near-empty sidewalk, then pushed open the shabby glass door of the bookstore. A tiny brass bell jingled overhead.

Inside, the space was dim, illuminated by tall shelves stuffed with worn volumes and random trinkets. A faint labyrinth of corridors opened beyond the entrance. She smelled dust, vanilla candles, and something akin to lotus leaves. Her footsteps fell softly against old carpet. Nobody waited behind the front counter. Every corner felt too dark, as though shadows pulsed with an awareness of their own.

She took a steadying breath. She had not come this far for nothing. The instructions, if that simple card could be called instructions, had said only that the Sanctuary entrance lay behind the store. An ordinary door some-where, presumably hidden. She had tested doorways in the last aisle, her mind thrumming with the same nervous energy she felt before stepping onstage. Before stepping into a vision.

She tried the first side passage. It led to a cramped reading nook stacked with antique dictionaries. She slid her palm over the wall. Nothing. She circled back, scan-ning for a seam or an arch that might hide a door. Her fingers grazed rows of worn book spines. Then she noticed a beam of light from beneath a tattered hanging tapestry in the corner.

Candle glow pulsed through the faded red cloth. She reached out and lifted the corner, heart pounding. A black-lacquered door stood behind it, slightly ajar. The faintest trace of candle smoke curled from the crack below, beckoning her inside. She exhaled once, bracing, and stepped through.

The air changed the moment she crossed the threshold. The temperature dropped. It was as if she had passed from the normal hum of the city into another dimension. Her ears popped slightly, and the overhead lighting vanished, replaced by a line of tall, taper candles along the walls. She could not hear the muffled bookstore music anymore, and the quiet felt so complete that her own breath echoed in her ears.

She moved forward, one careful step after another. The corridor stretched longer than any building in Chinatown had a right to accommodate. Something about the geometry tilted. She fought the urge to turn back. If there was any chance of understanding her gift, of learning more about her place in the web of seers, it had to start here. Even so, fear coiled in her belly.

Mirrors lined the narrow hallway, tall and ornate, each in a different frame. Some were gilded and scrolled with intertwined leaves. Others were chipped, with tarnished edges. She caught her reflection in the first one on the left. The figure peering back at her looked too pale, her eyes too large, her shoulders stiff with tension. She pivoted to glance at another mirror on her right. There her reflection seemed half-blurred, features out of alignment, as if captured in the middle of shifting shape. She swallowed hard and kept walking.

Her foot scuffed against the concrete floor. Candle wax dripped in languid rivulets across iron holders. As she passed the second pair of mirrors, an unsettling feeling of being watched slithered up her spine. She felt eyes on her, but every time she glanced at a mirror, it showed only her own image, distorted or shimmering, yet undeniably hers.

Halfway down, the corridor took a subtle turn, and the mirrors began to curve inward, forming a shadowy funnel that led to a single chamber. She paused at the bend. She listened. No footsteps, no murmurs, nothing but her heart thudding against her rib cage.

She spoke aloud, her voice nearly lost to the silence. "Hello?"

No answer. Only the flutter of candle flames.

Her entire body tensed. She pressed on, crossing the boundary into the final stretch. The space opened wider, revealing a circular room. Its walls were covered in even more mirrors, forming a mosaic of reflections that glinted in the candlelight. And there, at the far side of the chamber, stood a man.

Lucien Grey.

He was not moving, nor was he surprised to see her. He watched her the way a sculptor might survey a statue that had finally stepped off its pedestal. His posture was poised, one hand resting lightly behind his back as if he had been expecting her for some time. Pulsing light caught the angle of his cheekbones, accentuating an inhuman beauty that stirred both wonder and alarm in her. His hair was pale, almost silver in the uncertain light. His clothing appeared modern enough, dark slacks, a fitted coat, but something timeless clung to him, like a memory of an older era.

She swallowed. Part of her wanted to speak, but the words tangled inside her. The quiet pressed in, making her shoulders tense. Instinct told her this man was not just another seer. He radiated an authority that made the candles seem dim in comparison. The hairs on her arms prickled in response.

He inclined his head slightly, a greeting both polite and unnerving.

Pouring every bit of courage into a calm front, she stepped fully into the chamber. An arch of slender candles burned behind him, forming a shape that reminded her of a half-drawn circle. At her arrival, a wave of air seemed to ripple across the room, brushing against her ankles as though traveling from the corridor behind her to the place where he stood.

Still, he did not speak. The silence swelled, thick with unspoken promises. She forced herself to take another step. The reflections danced across his face. He shifted his gaze slowly, as if confirming something only he perceived. Her pulse soared into her throat. It was as if he could see beyond the surface of her skin, directly into the storm of her mind, her visions, her half-formed nightmares.

Her voice came out in a tremor. "Are you Lucien Grey?"

He offered the barest suggestion of a smile. It was dark, amused, neither friendly nor hostile. "I am."

Her throat went dry. She realized she had known the answer the moment she laid eyes on him. She had seen him in dreams that blurred truth with premonition. She was certain he already knew that.

"It feels like the air is bending," she said softly, glancing at the mirrored walls. Her own reflection repeated a hundred times, each blink distorting her posture. "Like none of this is in the right shape."

He looked unconcerned, as though the tilting reality was exactly what he intended. Silence returned. She struggled to keep her composure.

"I came because..." She paused, tasting her own uncertainty. She almost said, "I came because someone left a card," but the weight of everything she had felt, from cryptic warnings to half-buried longing, was too heavy for such a small explanation.

She tried again. "I want answers." Her voice vibrated with all the nights spent wondering if she should accept or reject the invites to these secret enclaves. "About who I am. What I can do."

Candlelight illuminated him from behind, drawing a bright halo around his figure. He shifted closer, his footsteps eerily silent on the stone. With each measured step, an invisible tension coiled, like a string pulling her in. She suddenly remembered the times she had dreaded a presence in her dreams, a shape that lingered just outside her field of vision. Now there he stood, no longer separated by the haze of sleep.

His dark-lashed eyes swept her face as he came to a stop. The silence stretched on, and she noticed the subtle curve of his mouth. It was a smile that held knowledge she did not yet possess. For some reason, heat prickled in her chest, a conflicting tangle of adrenaline and awareness. She clenched her hands at her sides, ignoring the shaky feeling in her fingertips.

"You are searching for your place among us," he said quietly. His tone was cultured, each syllable precise. "Sanctuary was once a refuge. Now it is a shadow of what it was. But you, Ivy Lewis, are not here for the architecture." His gaze darted around the mirrored chamber. "You have come because the city hums with your gifts, and you can no longer deny it."

She opened her mouth, but no immediate words came. His certainty disturbed her. She wanted to protest that she had simply followed the card's instructions, that she could turn around at any moment if she chose. Yet she stayed. She recognized him. Even if she had never seen him in person until now, he was the impossible figure at the edge of her visions.

"How do you know my name?" She tried to keep her voice from breaking. The candlelight created a mosaic of wavering shadows along the mirrored floor. Each shadow seemed to move on its own.

He did not answer right away. Instead, he studied her eyes, as if searching for something in the flecks of color. Then he exhaled a low breath that felt like it brushed her skin. "You have been dreaming of me," he murmured, no hint of question in his tone. "I can feel it in the echoes you carry."

Her heart pounded. The truth in those seven words

made her insides clench. Yes, she had dreamt of him. She recalled his glance in the half-lit corners of her nightmares. She had tried to piece together stranger details: an invisible corridor, a presence whispering her name. It always ended before she could see his face clearly. Now she stood in front of him, reality merging with dream. She felt exposed, as though her mind had been on display for him to pick through.

She wet her lips. "Yes," she said, keeping her voice as steady as possible. The single word felt like surrender, but denial seemed pointless. A silent moment passed. The candle flames wavered, and something like satisfaction curved his mouth.

His voice was quiet, yet it resonated with the authority of a man certain of his place in the world. "Then let us confirm what you already suspect. Your power is not random. It is the shape of your future, a path you were born to tread."

Ivy swallowed. She thought of all the warnings she had brushed aside, the times she had reeled from a sudden vision of events yet to happen. She wondered if she was truly on the cusp of an explanation or stepping deeper into a labyrinth from which she might not return.

She felt a drop of sweat trickle along her temple. She drew in a breath, ready to question him further. Who was he to speak as though he knew her fate more clearly than she did? Before she could frame the words, Lucien reached out, and his fingertips hovered near hers, not quite touching.

He looked at her with an intensity that made her

stomach twist. She sensed the potential in that almost-contact, as though the air between her fingers and his belonged to a living thing. She did not move away. Her feet held their ground, even as her heart thrashed in her chest.

He dipped his head, his gaze never leaving her face. In the quiet of that chamber, her own breathing sounded too loud. She watched his lips form a smirk, darkly amused, as if they shared a secret no one else could understand. The mirrored walls caught the candlelight and trapped it around them, turning the entire chamber into a sphere of shimmering reflections.

"Let us wake you up properly," he said, his voice low, every syllable charged with the promise of revelations.

CHAPTER
SIX

THE CIRCLE REFORMS

I vy stepped forward, leaving behind the receding echoes of Lucien's earlier whisper. The corridor of mirrors stretched ahead, lit by narrow candles. A low hum coursed through the stones beneath her feet, as though the building itself thrived on quiet secrets. She told herself to remain calm, to fight back the tremor in her hands. She had come here willingly, but she had not foreseen just how disorienting it would feel to be led deeper into a labyrinth that defied normal architecture.

Lucien walked beside her with unhurried confidence, clothed in a dark coat that brushed against the tops of his polished shoes. It was difficult not to stare at him. Though his expression was schooled into a mask of mild amusement, there was a pull around him, a soft gravitational tug that made her want to edge closer. She tried not to succumb to that secondary pulse in her chest, the reflexive jolt of attraction that seemed to spark anytime he looked her way.

She glanced around warily. The hallway's reflective walls carried fragments of her own image in a kaleidoscope effect. She saw her eyes repeated at odd angles, her shoulders angled in on themselves as she walked. The waver of candlelight made every reflection shiver. She slowed her steps, worried she might trip if she kept staring, or perhaps worried she might see some vision not meant for her. A wave of dizziness brushed the edges of her senses. No. She needed to maintain focus. She was here to discover why this place felt so tailored for her arrival.

Lucien paused at a fork in the corridor and turned his face toward her. The silence amplified the sound of his soft exhale.

His voice came out smooth and low. "I know the mirrors leave you a bit uneasy," he said. "They take some getting used to." His gaze darted over her face, assessing, though she noticed the faintest curl at the corner of his mouth, as if he took delight in her unease.

Before she could form a clever reply, a faint murmuring rose from the passage ahead. It sounded like the whispers of many voices, each separate but weaving together in a tapestry of half-finished sentences. Lucien rested a hand lightly at her elbow. She stiffened. At that gentle pressure, she felt the same strange thrumming she had sensed earlier, the place's heartbeat pulsing through his touch.

"Come," he said, guiding her forward. "They are waiting."

She did not ask who they might be. She swallowed and

let him usher her around the corner. The hallway opened into a round vestibule draped in heavy burgundy tapestries. A cluster of people stood in small groups, holding objects that glistened in the candlelight, small bowls, reflective shards of glass, beaded ribbons. All went silent when Ivy and Lucien appeared. Their gazes held curiosity. No one seemed truly surprised to see her, though some wore guarded expressions.

A woman with cropped black hair stepped forward, wearing an exquisite robe embroidered with delicate threads that gleamed in spirals. She examined Ivy from head to toe. "So the rumor is true," she said in a poised tone. "You finally brought her to us, Lucien. Is she prepared?"

Ivy opened her mouth to speak, but Lucien answered first. "Prepared is a relative term, Selene," he said smoothly. The corners of his eyes crinkled in a half-smile. "She is open. That is what matters."

Without further acknowledgment, Selene turned on her heel and slipped away through an archway into a larger room. The others followed her lead, moving in a gentle current that left Ivy and Lucien alone for a moment. He faced her with a faint nod, then indicated that she should accompany him.

They emerged into a spacious chamber that reminded Ivy of a subterranean cathedral. Taper candles stood everywhere, emerging from tall wrought-iron stands. The ceiling curved into a dome, and every surface seemed etched with spiraling patterns reminiscent of waves and vines. The quiet weighed heavier here, as if they had stepped into an antechamber for ritual. Ivy's breath caught when she noticed how the domed overhead space was ringed by small circular mirrors, each turned at a distinct angle. The shifting candlelight created a mosaic of reflections high above.

At the chamber's center stood an unassuming wooden table, bare except for a single unlit oil lamp. Two men and a woman hovered near its edge, talking in low, musical voices that braided around each other's words. Ivy strained to understand their conversation, but each phrase seemed to be a riddle or a puzzle. Their whispers flowed from references to hidden gates, broken lines, and a tapestry of star patterns. It sounded like half of an incantation, or perhaps an incomplete set of instructions. She realized with surprise that they were not ignoring her but might be welcoming her presence in their own cryptic fashion.

A rustling sound stirred behind her. She turned and saw a boy leaning against one of the candle stands, silent as a statue. He could not have been more than fourteen, with messy hair falling across his forehead. In one hand, he held a charcoal pencil. In the other, a worn sketchbook. His gaze rested entirely on Ivy. A hint of discomfort threaded through her stomach.

Lucien's voice lowered. "Cassian, come here."

The boy approached, his footsteps barely audible on the flagstone floor. He opened the sketchbook, and Ivy exhaled a small gasp. She recognized her own face drawn in charcoal, her same worried eyes, the delicate arc of her brows, and even the tension in her lips. The accuracy was uncanny, capturing both her likeness and an emotion she did not know she wore outwardly.

"That is me," she said under her breath, struggling for composure. "When did you draw it?"

Cassian said nothing. He only looked at Lucien, who gave the boy an approving nod. Lucien slid a hand across the page. "He sketches what he perceives, often before events happen," Lucien said. "A moment in the future or a breath in the present. Sometimes it is less about time and more about glimpsing essence." He paused, then glanced at Ivy. "He sees things differently than the rest of us."

Ivy felt a lump form in her throat. The idea that Cassian had captured her face, her uncertainty and her raw questions, without her even noticing made her shiver. She gave Cassian a gentle, if nervous, smile. He lowered his gaze and quietly turned the page, revealing an impressionistic swirl of lines. It looked partly like a shifting skyline, partly like pointed flames.

Quietly, Cassian walked away. He found a seat near the far wall, tucking himself behind a low table. Ivy felt a pang of sympathy for him. He seemed both vulnerable and incredibly gifted, not unlike a younger version of the same confusion she felt in her own life.

"Come," Lucien said again, gesturing for her to slip deeper into the chamber. They navigated the edges of the space, stopping at a large mirror propped against the stone. Selene knelt there, running her fingertips over its surface as if seeking a hidden latch.

"Yes?" she asked, her voice reedy and low.

Lucien gestured for Ivy to approach. "It might be time for her to see," he said.

Ivy felt an uncomfortable twist in her gut. "See what?"

Selene's eyes turned toward Ivy. "Your reflection," she said, though the words hung in the air like an incomplete answer. "You are the reflection." She rose to her feet, her robe trailing behind her. The candlelight danced over its elaborate threadwork, revealing half-hidden symbols that shimmered with each step.

Ivy lingered, uncertain if she should kneel or speak. The mirror's surface was a smoky silver. It was large enough for her to see herself in, but the reflection wavered as if rippling water hid just beneath the glass. She inhaled, but the lights and shadows in the reflection unsettled her mind. She sensed a push-and-pull, not unlike the echoes of her own premonitions. A part of her wanted to lean in, to see if the glass would show her a future she had not yet let herself imagine. Another part wanted to yank her gaze away.

From behind her, Lucien set a reassuring palm at her shoulder. She resisted the wave of heat that climbed her spine from that single touch. When he spoke, his voice was subdued. "We call this sanctuary the heart of our Circle. It stands on a crossing of energies older than the city itself. We gather here to sharpen our gifts and learn from one another's experiences. Some of us glimpse the future, some of us bind illusions, and some interpret the murmurings beneath the city's breath."

She could feel his breath near her ear, and for an

uneasy instant, she was reminded that he was not simply a courteous guide. He was a man steeped in secrets and power that could pull her in if she let him. She remembered how easily he had stepped into her dreams, the way his image had hovered in half-lit corners of her mind. Now he was flesh and blood at her side, making an entire group of seers part like the tide to let him pass.

"How long has this existed?" she asked, letting her gaze drift from the mirrored walls to the others who lingered in quiet conversation.

He chuckled softly. "Longer than you think. We once spanned continents, with enclaves hidden in catacombs and ancient temples. Our ancestors were sought by the great empires of old. Some used seers to guide them in war, others in politics. We thrived only when we remained free from such entanglements. But as time passed, thirst for power corrupted many of our own. Betrayals carved deep wounds. The Circle tore itself apart."

A few onlookers drifted closer, curious about what Lucien would reveal next. Ivy felt the quiet permeate the chamber again. She found herself drawn closer to him, as if each word he spoke carried an old echo that made the air tremble.

His voice turned solemn. "We lost faith because we placed it in the wrong people." His gaze swept the room. Selene gave a subtle nod of agreement, and those near the table cast their eyes downward, as though acknowledging a haunting memory.

"But here you are, building it again," Ivy said. She

glanced around at the strange gathering. Regardless of the cryptic words and labyrinthine paths, she sensed genuine devotion. Even if some hearts were guarded, each person carried a reverent air. "You call this place a sanctuary."

He inclined his head. "Sanctuary from shame, from fear, from the outside world that ridicules what it cannot explain. And also sanctuary for deeper truths. We do not seek to hide forever, but we must strengthen ourselves before we attempt anything greater."

A pang of curiosity flared in her mind. She had come, in part, for answers, yet Lucien's explanation teased more questions. Something about the atmosphere, the stutter of fire and the silence of watchers, pressed down on her chest. "So why me?" she said, her voice trembling despite her best efforts to keep it steady. "You keep talking as if I belong here. I hardly know what I am."

Lucien shifted to face her fully, candlelight illuminating the sharp planes of his cheeks. The hush deepened to a near-silence, so profound that Ivy wondered if everyone waited on his reply. Yet no one interrupted. He reached for her hand, not demanding it but offering his open palm. After a breath's hesitation, she let his skin brush hers. A current of heightened sensation rippled along her arm. She recalled the countless times she had felt an inexplicable surge of energy when her visions seized her. Now, that same sense of possibility coiled and uncoiled at her fingertips.

He left a small pause before his answer, as though weighing how to speak it. Then his lips curled into a measured smile. A hint of anticipation plucked at the edges of every nerve in Ivy's body.

"Because you're the disruption we've been waiting for."

CHAPTER

SEVEN

QUESTIONS OF LOYALTY

Ivy strained to hear the gentle chime of her shop's doorbell, half-expecting Ethan to stride in at any moment with another barrage of questions. Instead, only a few idling cars rolled by outside, accompanied by the muffled shouts of delivery drivers on the foggy sidewalk. The candles on her counter cast unsteady light across the rows of tarot decks. She felt restless. Ever since she had returned from the Sanctuary and met Lucien Grey, her life had started moving faster than any of the visions inside her head.

Robin offered a lopsided smile from behind the register. "You're going to pace a hole in the rug," she said, gesturing to the worn path Ivy's anxious footsteps had carved. "If you need to close early, I can handle the last readings on my own."

Ivy shook her head. "I'm fine. Seriously." Her voice sounded hollow to her own ears. In truth, she felt anything but fine. She wanted to call Ethan, to check in, but he had shut himself off after they last spoke. She had barely reached him the day before, and when she tried again this morning, the call went to voicemail. He had answered only once, his tone clipped as though something weighed on him. He said he had "work to do" and ended the conversation with a noncommittal promise to see her soon.

Robin exhaled and let the silence stretch. Finally, she glanced at their phone. "I need to prep some new listings online. Yell if you need backup." She disappeared into the storage room, leaving Ivy to her thoughts.

A fresh wave of tension curled in her chest. Her aunt Cassandra, too, had been vague all week. The older woman had refused to share details of her private meetings, dropping just enough hints to make Ivy's curiosity flare. Ivy wanted answers, but every time she demanded them, Cassandra told her, "You need to trust the process." Ivy hated cryptic responses. Lately, cryptic answers felt like the only language anyone around her knew how to speak.

Late in the afternoon, after Robin wrapped up the final reading and left for the day, Ivy locked the door and sat behind the counter. The overhead light drew her gaze to the row of crystals and charms displayed for customers. Her gaze snagged on the dark reflection of a mirror perched on the wall, only half-uncovered. An involuntary shudder rocked through her. Mirror scrying had always made her uneasy, but it was far worse now that Lucien Grey haunted her dreams. The entire city felt charged with static each time she thought of him.

A knock on the door jarred her out of her thoughts. She rose, heart kicking. She peeked through the glass and saw Cassandra standing outside, her collar flipped against the chill. Ivy hurried to let her in.

Her aunt stepped inside and brushed invisible dust from her flowing coat. "I hoped I'd catch you before you closed," she said. Her posture was tense, as though she had run out of patience in the last hour.

Ivy folded her arms. "I'm guessing you didn't just come for a tea refill."

Cassandra's lips curved faintly, though no real amusement shone in her eyes. She moved to the corner of the shop where a comfortable couch sat beneath a row of old dream-interpretation guides. After a moment's hesitation, Ivy joined her, the echoes of the day's readings hovering like stale incense.

"I went to lunch with Ethan this afternoon," Cassandra said. She tapped the end of her scarf, a habitual gesture that revealed her nerves. "He has been investigating again."

Ivy's eyebrows shot up. "Investigating what?"

"You can guess." Cassandra's gaze turned to the unlit candle near Ivy's elbow. The slender wick had burned down to nothing, much like Ivy's peace of mind. "He's been researching the old Seer's Circle, the one that fell apart decades ago. Every search led him back to one man. Grey."

At Lucien's name, Ivy felt a surge of heat behind her breastbone. "He's fixated on Lucien?"

Cassandra nodded. "He's worried. He's also determined to protect you from something he doesn't understand. I warned him he might be chasing a ghost, and ghosts don't appreciate being cornered. But I doubt he'll stop."

Ivy's heartbeat rattled in her ribs. She could imagine Ethan hunched over his laptop, scouring forums and combing through arcane references, trying to unravel the secrets she had barely begun to learn. "Why didn't Ethan tell me himself?"

Cassandra's expression softened. "He's planning to speak with you tonight, I believe. Just be aware he discovered enough to realize how dangerous Lucien might be. He's going to demand answers, Ivy. Be ready."

Ivy breathed in the warm, cinnamon-scented air and tried to calm the din inside her mind. She recalled the way Ethan's voice had turned strange on the phone earlier, as though he were holding back a thousand questions. "Thank you for letting me know."

Cassandra nodded and reached for Ivy's hand. "I can't tell you how to feel," she whispered. "But be cautious. You're precious to many people, including me. Don't give that power away lightly. Keep your heart clear, no matter which path you choose."

A hint of defensiveness rose in Ivy. She longed to snap that her heart was her own business, but her aunt's genuine worry subdued her. Instead, she murmured a quiet goodbye as Cassandra left. Then she closed the shop, her pulse thrumming with a new tension as she imagined Ethan on her doorstep. She sensed that tonight would change something between them.

Night fell early. By the time Ivy tidied the front room and collected her scattered notes, the streetlamps glowed in the growing mist. An hour later, she paced the length of her small kitchen at home, the overhead bulb casting dim shadows. She had brewed a pot of chamomile tea but found no taste for it. A restless, charged sense of anticipation clung to her every breath.

Finally, another knock came. She rushed to open the door. Ethan stood in the hallway, wearing a dark jacket zipped against the damp night. A draught followed him as he stepped into the apartment. His eyes locked on hers immediately, searching for something, maybe the same sense of uncertainty that lived in her chest.

He set his leather messenger bag on the nearest chair. "We need to talk," he said, his voice low.

She swallowed. "I know."

Without ceremony, he pulled a folded piece of paper from his pocket and handed it over. She saw references to archived library files. Her gaze skimmed a handful of blurred lines. Grey's name was scrawled repeatedly. Terms like *old rites, mass betrayal,* and *records missing* loomed like ominous signposts.

"I spent the last two days digging," Ethan said. "Everything points to Lucien Grey as a central figure in some ancient seer network that ran through the city. People wrote about him like he was a legend, even decades ago."

Ivy placed the page on her small dining table. Her stomach churned. "And Cassandra told me you met with her."

Ethan nodded, running a hand through his hair. "Yes.

She told me not to chase ghosts. That Lucien and others like him might be more dangerous when cornered." His gaze turned to Ivy's face. "But I can't just walk away when I see you turning deeper into this circle. I need to know, what are they asking from you?"

His words cut through the quiet. Ivy recognized this moment as the confrontation she had dreaded for weeks. She braced herself, forcing her shoulders not to tighten. "They're not exactly asking me to sign a contract, if that's what you mean," she said, aiming for a wry tone. "They see me as part of some new possibility for seers like them. They told me I'm chosen, that I have a power they want."

Ethan's jaw clenched. "That's exactly how cults operate. They single you out, feed you a grand destiny, and coax you to rely on them until you can't break free. I've reported on manipulative groups before. It always starts with flattery and ends with loss."

Heat flared in Ivy's cheeks. She pictured Lucien's calm, hypnotic eyes. A part of her bristled, not at Ethan's concern but at the assumption that she was too naive to see danger for herself. "So you think I'm too gullible to notice manipulation? Maybe it's better than pretending I'm not who I am." Her voice rose, surprising even herself.

Ethan fixed her with a stare that blazed with frustration and worry. "You think I'm dismissing you? No. I believe in you. But that's why I'm terrified. Lucien Grey is no ordinary man. You said that yourself. And now they want you to join them."

"Because I have these visions that nearly tore me apart," Ivy shot back. "And they're the only ones who didn't call me crazy for it. Even you wrote an article questioning me."

He winced at that reminder. "I was doing my job. I didn't know the whole story then."

"But you do now?" She let out a short laugh. "Countless nights, I've felt so alone, stuck between nightmares and the real world. They're offering me a place to belong, a sanctuary. And you're telling me to walk away."

Silence pressed between them, thick and charged. Ivy studied his gaze, that hint of yearning battling with his protective anger. Her chest felt too tight. Every piece of her wanted to melt into him, to free herself from the web of tension and questions. At the same time, she resented the implication that her search for answers made her a fool.

She forced her voice to steady. "I know it looks like I'm following Lucien blindly, but I barely trust him. I sense he's hiding more than he shares. Yet I also sense that he understands parts of me you are scared to look at."

Ethan's eyes sparked at that final remark. He reached for her arm, his fingers warm around her wrist. "I'm scared to lose you," he said bluntly. "I feel you slipping away into a world I can't see. Every day, I look for facts, for a rational explanation, and I keep coming up short. Everything leads back to some ancient ghost named Grey, and I don't know how to protect you from that."

She felt a pang of sympathy, her anger softening at the raw edge in his voice. "I'm not asking you to solve my visions," she whispered. "Just don't treat me like I'm broken."

His grip on her wrist tightened slightly, a gentle,

desperate gesture. "Maybe I'm more afraid that I'm the broken one," he admitted, his voice barely above a whisper. "I can't keep up with your world."

They stood close enough that she could feel the heat of his body against hers. His eyes glimmered with genuine longing, a longing that resonated in her own chest. A pulse of silence stretched. Then, with a tentative slowness, he raised his free hand and brushed his fingertips along her cheek. She leaned into the warmth.

The tension that had crackled between them shifted, transforming into a different kind of charge. She noticed the slight tremble in his shoulders as though anticipation coiled inside him. Guilt, regret, and desire mingled in the silence as her breathing deepened.

Their next exchange of words vanished in a soft collision of mouths. His lips met hers tentatively, as if testing the space between condemnation and comfort. The kiss stirred a fire at the pit of her stomach, one that had been building through all their arguments and half-truths. Ethan's hand slid around her waist, pulling her closer. She curled her arms around his neck, letting the frustration dissolve into a fervent need to be seen and understood.

They broke apart for a moment, breathless. She studied the shadows in his eyes, finding her reflection in them, filled with all the fear and hope she couldn't put into words. "Stay," she whispered, barely trusting herself to speak louder. "Please, stay."

He answered by pressing his lips to her throat, a silent vow that he wasn't going anywhere. They stumbled backward in unison, guided by an unspoken need. Her back hit the small kitchen table, rattling the teacups left untouched from earlier. She parted her lips to apologize, but Ethan silenced her with another kiss that made her forget everything but the warmth of his arms.

They moved to the bedroom, shedding tension and breath in murmurs. The faint glow of the bedside lamp lit the curve of his shoulder and the determined line of his jaw. She realized how long she had wanted this connection, how many times she had dreamed of anchoring herself to him when visions threatened to swallow her whole. Now, with each tug at a zipper and each whisper of clothing against skin, she felt her anxieties slip away.

He pulled her close. She felt the thud of his heartbeat against her chest. Need mixed with tenderness in his gaze as he brushed her hair aside, revealing the curve of her neck. The city's distant hum provided a steady roar in the background, car engines and foghorns weaving into a lullaby that lulled them further into each other.

Their lips found familiar places, the hollow of her collarbone, the soft slope of his shoulder. His breath caught on her name, and she arched against him, welcoming his warmth and surrendering to her own desire. In that moment, no illusions or cult warnings could intrude. There was only the raw, undeniable intimacy binding them. Their bodies aligned in a slow, purposeful rhythm, each movement a confession of trust and longing. She felt the last barrier of caution erode as she gave herself to the moment, her heart pounding in her ears.

When it ended, they pressed together in the quiet aftermath, breathing in tandem as if they had discovered a singular pulse. She closed her eyes, letting his heartbeat lull her. The city lights blinked against the drawn curtains. Ethan's hand laced with hers, a small but certain promise.

They stayed like that for a while, tangled in the sheets and each other's arms, sharing silent truths they had danced around for weeks. Ivy rested her head on his shoulder, her mind free of the chaotic tangle that usually filled it. For once, she felt ground underfoot, a steadiness that had nothing to do with visions or secret circles.

EIGHT

THE SPACE BETWEEN

The first light of dawn was a shy, apologetic gray that filtered through the blinds of Ivy's bedroom, striping the rumpled sheets and the still air with pale light. Ivy woke slowly, her consciousness drifting up from a deep, dreamless sleep, the first she'd had in what felt like an eternity. She was aware, first, of warmth. A steady, living heat pressed against her back, and the solid weight of an arm was draped protectively over her waist.

Ethan.

The memory of the previous night surfaced not as a chaotic flood, but as a series of quiet, potent stills. The raw desperation in his voice as he'd stood in her living room, the fear in his eyes mirroring her own. The way their argument, sharp and full of jagged edges, had collapsed under the weight of a much older, deeper current of feeling. The collision of their mouths had been less a kiss and more a confession, of fear, of longing, of a desperate need to find an anchor in a world that had come untethered.

She shifted slightly, and Ethan stirred behind her, his breath warm against her neck. His arm tightened its hold, pulling her closer against his chest as if he feared she might dissolve with the morning mist. She closed her eyes, allowing herself this one stolen moment of peace. Here, tangled in the sheets with him, the world felt blessedly simple. There were no seers, no prophecies, no manipulative men with eyes like winter frost. There was only the steady rhythm of his breathing and the comforting solidity of his body next to hers.

But the peace was a fragile veneer. Beneath it, the unresolved questions still hummed. Their intimacy had been a truce, not a resolution. They had found solace in each other's bodies, but their minds were still on opposite sides of a vast, fog-shrouded chasm.

"You're awake," Ethan murmured, his voice thick with sleep. He pressed a soft kiss to her shoulder blade, a gesture so tender it made her heart ache.

"I am," she whispered, not turning to face him yet. She kept her gaze fixed on the way the light played across the grain of her wooden dresser. "Did you sleep?"

"Eventually," he admitted. "After I was sure you weren't going to bolt from the room screaming again." A hint of a tease was in his tone, but it was underscored by genuine concern. He traced a slow, gentle pattern on her hip with his thumb. "You were really scared last night, Ivy."

The memory of the shadow in her living room, the burning glyph, the suffocating terror of her vision, sent a faint tremor through her. "I was," she said. "It felt like the dream followed me out. Like a piece of it was still clinging to me."

He was quiet for a long moment. She could feel him choosing his words, navigating the delicate landscape of the morning after. "We need to talk about it," he said finally, his voice losing its sleepy edge and taking on the familiar, focused tone of the journalist who needed all the facts. "About all of it. Lucien. The Circle. What they're doing to you."

Ivy's stomach tightened. The fragile peace shattered. She knew he was right, but every part of her recoiled from the conversation. How could she explain the inexplicable pull of the Sanctuary when she barely understood it herself? How could she describe the chilling allure of Lucien Grey without sounding like she was betraying Ethan, betraying herself?

She rolled over to face him, pulling the sheet up to her chin. His blue-gray eyes were clear and serious, the rumpled state of his dark hair the only sign of the night's disarray. He looked at her with an intensity that was both loving and analytical, and she felt a familiar pang of being a puzzle he was determined to solve.

"I know we do," she said, her voice small. "But I don't know where to start. Every time I try to explain it, I feel like I'm speaking a different language. You see a cult, a manipulative group preying on the vulnerable. And I..." She trailed off, searching for the right words. "I see people who are just as lost and scared as I am. I see a place where I'm not the only one who sees things that shouldn't exist.

For the first time in my life, Ethan, I'm not the odd one out. I'm just one of them."

The confession hung in the air, raw and vulnerable. She watched his expression, saw the conflict in his eyes. He wanted to understand, she knew he did. But his logic, his need for proof and tangible evidence, was a fortress.

"One of them?" he repeated softly. "Ivy, these 'people like you' are being led by a man who haunts your dreams. Being understood shouldn't come at the cost of your safety."

"Maybe safety is an illusion," she countered, a touch of frustration creeping into her voice. "Maybe the only real choice is what kind of danger you're willing to live with."

He flinched, and she immediately regretted her words. That was a line of thinking Lucien would approve of. She saw the hurt in his eyes and reached out, her fingers brushing his cheek. "I'm sorry. I didn't mean it like that. I just, I'm so tired of being torn."

He captured her hand, lacing his fingers through hers. "I know. And I'm sorry too. I don't want to fight with you. I just want to protect you."

"I know you do," she whispered. And that was the heart of the problem. His love was a shield, but sometimes it felt like a cage. The Circle, for all its dangers, offered a key.

A resolve began to form in her mind, solidifying out of the morning's emotional fog. She couldn't keep living like this, with her life split into pieces. She couldn't have this intimacy with Ethan while hiding the true depth of the world she was stepping into. And she couldn't keep leaning on Robin without giving her the full context for her fear. They were her found family, her anchors. They deserved the whole truth, no matter how terrifying it was.

She squeezed his hand. "Okay," she said, her voice gaining a new firmness. "Let's talk. But not just us. I want Robin here too. If we're going to figure this out, we need the whole team."

Ethan's eyebrows lifted in surprise, but then a slow nod of agreement followed. "Okay," he said, his voice mirroring her resolve. "The whole team."

A few hours later, the three of them were gathered in the back room of The Oracle's Eye. The shop was closed for the day, a hand-lettered sign on the door reading "Closed for Inventory." It was a lie, but a necessary one. The energy in the room was too fragile for interruptions.

The air smelled of old paper, dried lavender, and the strong, dark-roast coffee Ethan had insisted on grabbing on their way over. Ivy sat on a worn velvet armchair, a steaming mug cradled in her hands. Robin was perched on a tall stool, her colorful pixie cut a bright slash of defiance against the room's dusty, muted tones. Ethan stood by the window, arms crossed, his posture radiating a tense, protective energy as he watched the fog-draped street.

"Okay," Robin said, breaking the silence. She looked from Ivy's pale face to Ethan's rigid one. "What's going on? You both look like you've seen a ghost."

Ivy took a deep breath, the steam from her mug warming her face. "In a way, we have. Or at least, I have." She set the mug down on a stack of books beside her. "I asked you both here because you deserve to know everything. Not just the pieces I've been feeding you. The whole story. And it's a lot."

She began, her voice quiet but steady. She started with the meeting she'd had with Cassandra and Thalia, the one she had only partially described before, and her meeting with the circle. She laid it all out, every detail she had been holding close to her chest like a painful secret.

Ethan finally turned from the window, his face grim. "This is what I was afraid of, Ivy. This isn't a community. It's a power grab. He's not trying to help you trying to use you. You're the key to whatever dangerous game he's playing."

"I know it looks that way," Ivy said, her voice pleading. "And part of me knows you're right. But it's more complicated than that."

Robin found her voice. "Okay. Nope. Absolutely not," she said, standing and beginning to pace the small room. "You are not going to be the battery in some magical doomsday device for a creepy, centuries-old cult leader. We are shutting this down."

Ivy couldn't help but let out a small, watery laugh at their fierce, protective loyalty. "I don't think it's that simple, Robin."

"Then we make it simple," she insisted, stopping in front of her. "You are not a tool. You are not a weapon. You are our friend. And we're are not letting him have you."

Ethan squeezed her shoulder, his grip firm and reassuring. "Robin's right," he said, his voice a low, determined rumble. "We're not going to let that happen."

Ivy looked at their faces, Robin's, blazing with protective fire, Ethan's, etched with a fierce, loving resolve. A wave of gratitude so intense it almost brought her to her knees washed over her. They were her anchors. They were her truth.

And yet.

Even as she felt their love wrapping around her like a shield, a small, traitorous part of her felt a pang of loss. They saw the danger, the manipulation, the horror. But they couldn't see the other side of it. They couldn't feel the profound, earth-shattering relief of being *seen*.

"I know you want to protect me," she said, her voice trembling. "And I love you both so much for it. But you have to understand what it feels like. All my life, I've felt like I was broken. My parents, my teachers, even my psychiatrist, they all tried to fix me, to explain away the things I saw. They treated my gift like a symptom of a disease."

She looked down at her hands, at the faint, shimmering glyph on her wrist. "The people in the Sanctuary, they're the first people who have ever looked at me and not seen something wrong. They see something powerful. It was terrifying, yes. But it was also the first time I felt whole. It was the first time I had a name for the strange, chaotic thing that lives inside me."

Her gaze lifted, pleading with them to understand. "Lucien is dangerous. I know that. But he's also the only person who has ever looked at the full force of my power and not flinched. He's not afraid of it. He's not afraid of *me*. And there's a part of me, a part I hate, that is drawn to that. To the idea of not having to hide or shrink myself. To the idea of finally, finally being understood."

The confession left her breathless, exposed. She had given voice to the secret, shameful conflict in her own heart. The pull toward the light of her friends' love, and the gravitational tug of Lucien's darkness.

Ethan knelt in front of her, taking both of her hands in his. His eyes were shining with an emotion she couldn't quite name, not anger, not pity, but a deep, sorrowful empathy.

"I understand," he said, his voice so soft it was almost a whisper. "I understand wanting to be seen for who you are. He sees your power, yes. But he doesn't see *you*. He doesn't see the woman who leaves half-finished cups of tea all over her apartment, who hums off-key when she's nervous, who has more compassion in her little finger than that entire Circle has in its centuries of history. That's the woman I see. That's the woman I..." He stopped, his throat working. "That's the woman I'm fighting for."

Tears streamed freely down Ivy's face now, but they were tears of a different kind. Not of fear, but of a heart-breaking, overwhelming love. She leaned forward, resting her forehead against his, and let out a shuddering sob.

Robin came to kneel beside them, wrapping an arm around Ivy's shoulders and squeezing tight. The three of them stayed like that for a long time, a small, defiant island in a sea of encroaching darkness.

The conversation had changed nothing and every-thing. The dangers were still there. Lucien was still waiting. Ivy was still torn, her heart a battlefield for two conflicting desires.

But as she knelt there, buffered by the two people who formed the core of her world, she felt a shiver of something new. Not a solution. Not a plan. But a quiet, fierce resolve. She didn't know which path she would have to take. She didn't know if she could save her city, her friends, or herself.

She only knew she would not be a pawn in anyone's game. Not Cassandra's, not Ethan's, and not Lucien's. The choice, when it came, would be hers alone. And in the charged, silent space between her two worlds, she began to gather her strength.

NINE

THE RITE OF INK

I vy lingered outside the heavy wooden door in a rarely used corridor of the Sanctuary, her shoulders tense and her heart drumming a steady beat in her ears. She had received Lucien's invitation earlier that morning in the form of a handwritten note slipped beneath the shop's door. There were no exact details, just directions to come alone after sunset. She had not told Ethan. A pang of guilt clung to her, but curiosity and something deeper pulled her onward.

The corridor was lit by half a dozen candles protruding from tall iron sconces. Their glow shimmered across the walls, creating dancing patterns on the stone floor. Ivy inhaled the air, laced with the faint scent of incense and aged leather. Her pulse hammered harder than it should. She rarely ventured into this remote wing of the Sanctuary. The quiet felt heavier here, as though this part of the labyrinth harbored secrets that even the more public areas had never touched.

She lifted her hand to knock. Before her knuckles met wood, the door swung open from inside. Lucien stood in the entrance. He looked almost ethereal in the candlelight, wearing a long coat of dark silk that whispered around his frame. His pale eyes found hers at once, heavy with questions and promises in that single glance. No formal greeting passed his lips. His gaze and a faint tilt of the head were enough to beckon her in.

She stepped into a circular chamber that smelled of herbs and burning resin. The walls were lined with dark tapestries depicting shapes, perhaps symbolic, perhaps protective. In the center stood a low wooden table, and on it lay a small ceremonial bowl, several bundles of cloth, and an array of ink bottles in gleaming metal holders. Arranged around the table were four other individuals: Selene, her dark braid coiled at her neck, Cassian, half-hidden behind his ever-present sketchbook, and two older members Ivy did not recognize. Each wore a robe trimmed in intricate lines and sigils.

A silence spread across the group as Ivy took in the scene. Her stomach fluttered at the sight of the inks. She suspected the Marking might be a tattooing ritual. The Circle was nothing if not steeped in tradition. She had seen glimpses of other rites, but those had been subdued or shared in passing conversation. This felt different. It felt personal, as though it would bind her to something irreversible.

Lucien extended his hand toward the center of the chamber. "Welcome, Ivy." His voice was low, almost gentle, and it made the hair on her arms lift. "Tonight, we gather for the Rite of Ink. It is an ancient devotion to the gifts we carry, meant to honor and focus our abilities."

She glanced at Selene, who offered a small nod. Cassian peeked up from beneath the hood of his robe, his intense stare lingering on Ivy's face. She did not see judgment there, but rather a strange empathy, as though he knew a secret he could not verbalize. The older two members murmured their greetings, and one stepped forward to arrange the cloth on the table.

Ivy shifted her weight between her feet. She thought of Ethan for a moment, wondering if she had made the right choice in coming here without telling him. Something in her heart said she needed to keep part of this journey to herself. Perhaps she feared his reaction. Perhaps she did not want to mix her blossoming feelings for him with the intensity that Lucien brought into her life. Still, guilt twisted inside her.

Lucien's voice drew her attention from her thoughts. "Each participant offers a piece of their essence to the ink. It binds intention to form." He gestured at the small bottles arranged in a semi-circle. Her gaze darted over them: black ink, dark green, deep violet, and others that shimmered in the candlelight. "When it is placed beneath your skin," Lucien continued, "it will represent your commitment, not only to your gift but to yourself. That is the pillar on which the old Circle was built."

He moved closer, and she felt the distinct warmth that always accompanied him, a presence that slid under her defenses if she lingered too near. "Are you prepared?" he asked. There was a note of challenge in his tone.

She swallowed. "What exactly will happen to me once it's done?"

"The glyph you receive will reflect what resides in your visions, your unique power, and the future only you can shape. I cannot promise it will be painless, but the pain is part of the binding. It forces clarity." His expression softened. "You may see images. Perhaps you will glimpse the faces of those who came before you. They often greet a new thread in the tapestry."

"I see," she breathed. A subtle panic edged her thoughts. She feared losing herself to a torrent of visions, but she also felt drawn to the possibility of understanding them better.

Selene approached. "We will guide you. You are not alone in this, though the vision that emerges belongs to you."

A slight tremor touched Ivy's hands as she removed her jacket and placed it on a nearby stool. Beneath, she wore a simple sleeveless top. The air was cool on her exposed arms, but she sensed an inner flush of anticipation. She took her place beside the table, where a narrow cushion had been placed for comfort.

Lucien produced a small, curved needle pen. The older seer next to him handed over the first bottle of ink. The color inside looked black at a glance, but when the candlelight struck the glass, a hint of gold shimmered beneath the surface. Lucien bent down so that his lips were near her ear. "Think carefully of your intention," he whispered. "Call it to mind, hold it in your breath. The Marking will reveal whatever hides in your depths."

Ivy exhaled slowly, centering on the one thing she desired above all else, to take control of her gift. No more confusion. No more frantic second-guessing. She yearned for a foundation within herself, one that did not require external validation. Perhaps that was selfish, but she could not deny what her soul craved, self-possession and clarity.

Lucien touched the tip of the needle pen to her upper arm. She flinched at the cold metal against her skin. He paused, waiting for her to nod. When she did, he pressed the needle in a controlled motion, his breath steady. She gasped as the first prick of pain bloomed, sharp, startling. The sting forced her to focus on every sensation, from the hiss of the candles to the warm pulse in her veins.

In that moment of heightened awareness, the air thickened. The chamber's walls seemed to fall away, leaving only a darkness laced with light. Ivy could not feel the stone beneath her knees, nor hear the rustle of cloth around her. Instead, she sank into a velvety black void where shapes emerged like ghosts. She saw a tall woman with hair like hers but streaked with silver, her eyes blazing with a fierce energy. She recognized her grandmother from old photographs. The lines of the woman's face were etched with a mixture of regret and hope.

Her grandmother's eyes pinned Ivy in place, but a gentle smile curved her lips. Ivy felt tears burn behind her own eyelids. She wanted to speak, to ask so many questions. One by one, more figures stepped from the shadows, each emanating an otherworldly glow. Some wore elaborate robes, others stood in plain clothes from times long past. She sensed these were ancestors or at least seers who had carried the mantle before her. They murmured voices of encouragement she could only half-hear, as if calling from the other side of a thick pane of glass.

She felt Lucien's needle trace another stroke of ink across her arm, and the vision shifted. A series of images poured through her, a tall spire wreathed in smoke, the ocean turning to glass atop a moonlit cove, a flash of mirrored corridors that reminded her of the first time she walked the Sanctuary's labyrinth. In each scene, a feeling of raw power wound around her heart, reminding her that these possibilities already lived inside. None was guaranteed, but each was a path she might take.

Her breath came in ragged pulls. Her grandma's face appeared again, close enough to touch. Ivy almost reached out, only to watch the woman turn away, dissolving into a pool of light. The next stroke of ink seared her back to consciousness. She gasped so hard that her body pitched forward. Selene's hands pressed lightly against her shoulders, steadying her.

"It is almost complete," Lucien said. His tone was calm, guiding her through the final lines that the needle etched.

Tears clung to her lashes. Her arm vibrated with pain. She barely registered the repetitive press of the needle now. Her focus was caught between the burn of the ink and the afterimages dancing behind her eyelids.

Finally, Lucien lifted the needle pen away. The chamber settled into silence. The candles seemed brighter, as though she had just surfaced from somewhere deeper than dream. She felt dizzy, the edges of her thoughts blurred. Cassian's pencil scratched across paper, capturing something he perceived in her expression. Selene and the others chanted a subdued phrase, their voices weaving through, finalizing the rite.

Lucien wrapped a thin strip of gauze around the fresh tattoo, tying it securely. Then he offered a hand to help her stand. Her legs shook as she rose, and he guided her to a tall mirror propped against the far wall. Even in the candlelight, she could see the faint red lines on her arm where the ink had been set. The gauze was mostly clear, revealing a newly drawn glyph, a spiral of curved lines intersecting at a central point, subtly reminiscent of a blooming flower and an open eye at once.

"This is your thread in the tapestry," Lucien told her, his voice quiet but charged. He reached out and ran his fingertip just above the gleaming black lines, careful not to disturb the tender skin. "Do not let anyone cut it."

Ivy's pulse throbbed in her ears. She was only half-aware that the others had backed away, giving her space. The glyph, although raw and slightly swollen, glimmered with a subtle glow under the candles, almost as if it had an internal light. She had never felt so bound to anything so quickly. A wave of emotion rushed through her. She could not name it. Gratitude, fear, maybe acceptance of herself in a way she had not allowed before.

For a moment, the lines wavered, the edges dissolving into a shimmer. She blinked, and the glow receded, leaving only the fresh black ink. With trembling fingers, she touched the bandage. She should have felt foolish, yet she did not. This was real. The slight sting in her arm proved it. Beyond that physical pain stretched an understanding. Something had changed inside her, irrevocably.

She inhaled a slow breath and lifted her gaze to Lucien in the mirror's reflection. His pale eyes were steady, trained on her every reaction. She remembered how easily he drew her into dangerous emotion, how his soft words had convinced her to come here tonight. Anger or resentment should have flared. He had manipulated her before. Yet, as she looked at him, all she felt was the echo of that vision, reminding her that she had chosen to be here. She chose to shape her gift rather than fear it.

A soft clinking noise made her glance aside. Selene was gathering the ink bottles, recorking them with care. Cassian tore a page from his sketchbook, which he handed to Lucien. Ivy did not see what he had drawn, but the slight crease in Lucien's brow suggested something unexpected. The older seers bowed their heads in acknowledgment that the ceremony was complete.

Ivy turned away from the mirror. Her arm felt warm, the occasional throb reminding her of each new line. She forced herself to step toward Selene and Cassian, offering a small nod of acknowledgement. They provided gentle smiles, though Cassian's gaze darted to her bandaged arm as though he was still analyzing the resonance of her mark.

Lucien angled his head and lowered his voice. "You did well. The Circle gains another tether to the future by way of your courage."

An uneasy flush touched Ivy's cheeks. "I hope courage is the correct word," she said quietly. She caught her reflection in the mirror one last time. She expected to see hesitation or regret, but her eyes were alight with something else, determination. A faint thrill coursed through her veins.

Selene motioned for her to follow, and the rest of the group led Ivy from the chamber, leaving Lucien behind to extinguish the candles. Ivy realized she would have to explain herself eventually, to Ethan, to Robin, to Cassandra. But not yet. Tonight was hers alone. She had chosen secrecy. Whether that choice was brilliant or disastrous was a question she would confront later. For now, she held the echoes of her grandmother's face in her mind, recalling how she had seemed so proud, so certain. It gave Ivy a delicate hope that scarred over her guilt.

They passed through another narrow corridor and ended in a smaller antechamber. Soft lamplight replaced the dancing flames, and a gray woven rug muffled their footsteps. Selene left to retrieve fresh bandages in case Ivy's bled through. Cassian slipped away, quiet as a shadow. The two older seers offered her polite farewells. Then Ivy was alone.

She examined the layered bandage on her arm. The initial sting had dulled to a manageable throb. Carefully, she peeled back a corner of gauze, curious. Beneath it, the glyph shone for the span of a heartbeat, an otherworldly gleam. She caught her breath, entranced. In a blink, it faded, sinking back to ordinary black ink. Her heart kicked against her ribs.

She closed the gauze again, trying to calm her thoughts. The Rite of Ink was complete. The part of her that had wavered between fear and doubt felt newly anchored by the design on her skin. She could not define where this road would lead, but one thing was certain. The mark had merged with her, forging a bond she sensed as a pulsing thread winding through her core. She brushed her fingertips over the bandage one last time. A whispered gratitude bubbled up in her throat, though she was not sure if she thanked Lucien, her grandmother, or something bigger that she could not name. With slow steps, she slipped out of the antechamber, leaving behind the lingering smell of ink and spiced resin.

In the candlelit corridor, she paused to inhale the quiet, settling the noise in her head. She knew she had crossed another threshold tonight. Even the quiet felt more resonant. She pressed her palm lightly over the fresh tattoo, letting that spark of warmth remind her that part of her future now lived in an etched symbol on her arm. She exhaled and walked onward. The glyph remained hidden, but she sensed it just beneath the bandage, a living current threaded through her being. It was a quiet vow, a promise forged in ink and intention, echoing every time her heart beat.

She did not look back through the labyrinth. She supposed Lucien was still in that chamber, extinguishing the last of the candles or studying Cassian's cryptic drawing. Perhaps he felt satisfied. Perhaps he yearned for something more. She did not know, and for the moment, she did not want to. Once she stepped into the night air, a gentle fog curled around her as if welcoming her back to the city's silence. The streetlamps glowed faintly, illuminating fine mist drifting across the pavement. Her breath quickened, and she rubbed her forearm to soothe the faint ache.

She would linger in this mingled feeling of fear and exhilaration a while longer. Beneath the gauze, the sigils and lines she had accepted into her body glowed for an instant in her mind's eye. She felt them connect to the old lines of lineage, latching onto a power that had been waiting for her to show up and claim it.

When she finally dared to peel the bandage again at home to clean the area, the design flashed softly. In the mirror's reflection, it almost pulsed like a heartbeat. Then the glow receded, leaving an ordinary tattoo behind. She traced the lines with delicate care, feeling echoes of that vision. The new mark felt alive in a way she could hardly describe.

She let the bandage fall closed. The glyph had faded to black, quiet and subtle, invisible to anyone if she wore a long sleeve. Yet she sensed that it would never truly fade, for it had embedded itself deeper than mere flesh, speaking more to her destiny than she cared to admit. She touched the mirror in front of her and saw no illusions, only an unsteady reflection of her own face.

But the connection remained, pulsing beneath her skin.

CHAPTER

TEN

A MESSAGE IN FIRELIGHT

Ivy slept fitfully. Her body felt warmer than usual, as if the heat of her dreams had seeped into her veins and refused to let go. In this dream, fire danced across every surface, licking up walls of rough stone and twisting across the floor in a vibrant dance that never quite consumed the space entirely. She stood in something that felt half real and half imagined, a corridor lit by flames rising from unseen torches. Each breath filled her lungs with the coppery tang of smoke.

Beyond the flare of embers, a figure emerged and walked toward her. She recognized Lucien Grey at once, his pale eyes reflecting the columns of flame. He wore his ageless composure with unsettling grace. Where others might have flinched from the heat, he merely allowed it to curl closer, edging toward the hem of his long coat. A faint smile played at the corner of his lips.

"You feel it, do you not?" he asked quietly, his voice steady over the crackle of flame.

Ivy's pulse pounded in her temples. She could not will herself to speak at first. She felt bound to watch, and to follow, no matter how every rational thought in her mind screamed that this was dangerous. After a moment, she managed to force out, "Feel what?"

His lips curved more fully, but the smile never reached his eyes. "The choice pressing against your heart. The city's future and your own are bound so tightly. One might claim they have always been the same. Yet you waver."

"I don't understand," she whispered, although part of her sensed that she did. She had spent weeks trying to align the life she had cherished, a life with Ethan, with her small Oracle shop, with the possibility of normal days, and this new pull from the Sanctuary, from Lucien, from a lineage she had never truly asked for. Even now, the heat in this dream felt more like a challenge than comfort.

"You will," Lucien murmured. The flames intensified around them, roaring in a sudden torrent. His face vanished behind the curtain of heat, though she still heard his voice. "All that remains is to decide which future is worth saving."

Ivy wanted to ask him if that meant one future had to be forsaken, but the dream shifted without warning. Light flooded her vision, scalding her senses until she bolted upright in her real bed, gasping for air. The room lay in darkness except for a faint glow that caught in the edges of her sight. She pressed a trembling hand over her racing heart. A dream, she told herself firmly. Only a dream. Yet the air smelled faintly of smoke, or perhaps that was her overactive mind.

Taking several steadying breaths, she glanced around her bedroom. The heavy curtains at her window glowed with the ambient light of the city, but something else shone near the bookshelf. She squinted, her throat still tight from the lingering terror. At first, she thought the reflection came from a candle outside, or maybe her neighbor's porch light. Then she realized a single book on her top shelf shimmered with a dull, golden hue.

Cassandra's old journal.

Ivy had accumulated several of her aunt's notebooks in recent weeks, gleaning the cryptic references they held. Still, she had never seen one glow of its own accord. Swallowing her apprehension, Ivy slid out of bed. The floor felt freezing beneath her bare feet. She half expected the plank to be hot, recalling the fire from the dream, but it was only cool wood, as mundane as it had ever been.

Yet nothing about the dream had felt mundane. Even awake, she could almost taste cinders on her tongue. She stepped toward the bookshelf, her heart hammering more with each step. The journal's cover was bound in browned leather, its corners reinforced by battered metal plates. Its spine bore no title, just a faint pattern of symbols Ivy had not deciphered. Tonight, it glowed with a muted heartbeat of light. She braced herself for a jolt of arcane energy, but her fingers only met smooth, warm leather.

She carried the journal back to her bed, set it on the rumpled sheets, and turned on the bedside lamp. A soft, sepia glow bathed the pages when she opened it. Most she had read weeks ago, scanning the old scribbles of Cassandra's mother, her own grandmother, and the subsequent generations of seers in her family. But the final ten pages had always appeared blank.

Ivy flipped past the earlier recordings of old rituals, references to mirror scrying, half-legible instructions for speaking with the spirit realm, vague warnings about illusions. When she reached the end, she frowned. The pages still seemed empty. Yet the cover continued to faintly shine, pulsing so faintly that she might have imagined it. Something about the emptiness tugged at her. She pressed her palm against the last page, her breath uneven.

A memory from earlier that month darted through her mind, Cassandra's remark about certain inks that vanished until exposed to fire or other forms of heat. Ivy's dream had shown her enough fire for several lifetimes. She slowly lifted her hand off the page. Without a second thought, she reached for the small candle on her nightstand, the kind she lit for soft illumination when she read. With a quick strike of a match, she brought the flame near the paper. She took care not to set the journal ablaze, though her pulse beat in her throat as if she was about to do exactly that.

At first, the page remained blank. She brought the candle closer, letting the page warm under the flame's proximity. Tiny lines of ink came into view. Ivy drew in a sharp breath as strands of text revealed themselves, faint and wavering like ghosts summoned from the beyond. She shifted the candle in small arcs, coaxing out the words until she could read them.

The Veiled One will see both futures, hers and the city's, and must choose which to save.

She stared at the sentence. Though it was short, it wielded a terrible weight, like it pinned her between two massive doors. Her mind spun with the echo of Lucien's voice in her dream, urging her toward a decision. She tried to read further, but the ink faded just below that line, leaving the rest of the page blank. No hints, no extra commentary. Only that single pronouncement.

Ivy heard her own breath hitch. There is no ignoring this, she thought. For weeks, random scraps of prophecy had drifted through different journals, none so direct. This statement felt like a final challenge. A chill slid down her spine. She closed the journal and pushed it away, as if physical distance might dull its impact. When her pulse returned to something resembling normal, she scanned her phone for the time. Nearly three in the morning. Calling Cassandra at this hour would get her a dozen scoldings and no real clarity. She chewed the inside of her cheek, hesitating. Then she tapped Robin's number. She doubted Robin slept at a normal hour anyway, especially after the past few days at the shop, which had turned into a flurry of intense readings and whispered conversations about the Sanctuary.

Robin picked up on the second ring. "Ivy?" Her usually bright, sarcastic voice sounded groggy but concerned. "It's late. Are you okay?"

Ivy clutched the phone tighter. "I had another dream," she whispered, steadying her voice as best she could. "And something else. That old journal Cassandra gave me, it glowed. There's a hidden passage. You mind coming over?"

She heard sheets rustling, then a rustle of fabric. She could picture Robin climbing off her couch or possibly out of bed, rummaging for shoes while balancing the phone on one shoulder. "I'll be there in ten minutes," she said. "Throw on some coffee."

"Sure," Ivy murmured. "Thank you." She ended the call, exhaling as if she had been holding her breath for hours.

She did not want to be alone with the memory of that dream. Lucien's presence in the flames still haunted her. She felt, for a moment, the echo of his hand on her wrist, the calm threat in his eyes.

In the kitchen, she turned on the light and started heating water for coffee. Despite the tension roiling inside her, every detail of her surroundings looked painfully ordinary, the clock ticking over the stove, the chipped mug left from her last cup of tea, a stray piece of chalk on the counter from the shop's signboard. She realized how much she wished she had a normal life, one where she did not anticipate that her own reflection might merge with somebody else's face. Yet she knew that was naive. Her arm still bore the Marking from the Sanctuary, the glyph that occasionally pulsed warm to remind her she had already stepped too far into a world that would never be normal again.

Robin arrived sooner than Ivy expected, wearing a long coat over plaid pajama bottoms and mismatched sneakers. Her hair was shaped into an uneven mohawk from sleep. She took one look at Ivy's face and sobered, setting down a small messenger bag on the table.

"All right," Robin said, her voice quiet. "Spill."

Ivy guided her to her bedroom, where the journal lay waiting on the bed. She grabbed the candle from the nightstand, demonstrating how the words reappeared when exposed to heat. Robin's eyes widened when she read the line.

The Veiled One will see both futures—hers and the city's—and must choose which to save.

"Veiled One," Robin muttered, running a hand through her hair. "That has to be you, yeah? Or at least that's what the Circle folks called you once, right? The one bridging visions?"

Ivy nodded, feeling the dread tighten in her chest. "Lucien implied something like this in my dream tonight. He said I would have to choose. As if only one can be saved."

Robin gently closed the journal. Her expression held a hint of anger on Ivy's behalf. "I hate how cryptic these prophecies always are. Why not put it plainly, you must do X or Y. Instead, they set you up for heartbreak."

Ivy sank onto the edge of her bed, shoulders slumped. She stared at the wavering candle, remembering Lucien's words about forging a path and choosing a future. "Maybe heartbreak is the point," she said softly. "Prophecies test you, right? I just, I don't know how to see my future as separate from the city's."

Robin rested a reassuring hand on Ivy's shoulder. "We'll figure it out. At least you aren't alone." They scanned the page again, as if hoping more words would reveal themselves. "Go on. Read it to me," she said. "Sometimes speaking it out loud helps."

Ivy lifted the book and read the faded sentence slowly, allowing each syllable to resonate. *"The Veiled One will see both futures, hers and the city's, and must choose which to save."* Her voice nearly shook by the end. The words felt final, a seal on whatever path she would have to take.

Robin let out an unsteady breath. "What if you can't separate them?" she asked, her voice breaking the silence. "Would that mean saving yourself might doom the city? Or saving the city, well, you get the idea."

Ivy swallowed hard. She remembered how, in her dream, the fire had threatened to swallow both. She realized she had never considered that one might need to burn so the other could thrive. It felt impossible to rationalize. She licked her lips, hesitating. Fear coiled in her gut. "Then maybe one has to burn," she whispered. Her eyes moved up to meet Robin's. "Even if it means losing everything else."

Those words hung there, potent as flame. She exhaled, pressing the journal shut. The candle sputtered behind them, leaving a tendril of smoke that curled into the air, echoing the unsettled truth in her heart.

CHAPTER
ELEVEN
ECHOES OF THE DEAD

I vy felt Cassandra's stare long before the older woman spoke. The tension in Cassandra's Nob Hill townhouse had expanded throughout the evening, vibrating between the polished banister and velvet drapes like a warning. Despite the dusky calm outside, Ivy could sense a charged readiness around them. She stood in the entryway, carefully shrugging off her coat. Candlelight played across the deep lines of Cassandra's face. The older woman had not said a word since Ivy arrived.

"Are you all right?" Ivy asked, stepping closer. She tried to keep her voice soft, aware that any sudden noise felt too loud for these walls.

Cassandra's sharp gaze darted across Ivy's features, measuring and guarded. "We cannot ignore what you saw," she replied, pressing her hands together. She wore a turtleneck sweater in black, the sleeves rolled to her elbows. Two silver bangles rattled on her wrist. "Nor can we ignore what the mirror said."

Ivy swallowed. She thought she had grown used to cryptic references about visions or parted veils, but Cassandra's words still jolted her. "Which mirror do you mean?"

A subtle tremor worked through Cassandra's posture, as if the woman was uncertain about this decision. "We have a mirror here," she began, "from a time before I can clearly remember. It was your grandmother's. My mother's." She let out a breath. "She died under tragic circumstances."

Ivy nodded, locking her arms around herself. There was a prick of frustration beneath her skin. That single statement felt like a puzzle. So many details about their family, hidden behind Cassandra's guarded remarks. "You never told me she owned a special mirror."

Cassandra gave a wry smile. The candlelight softened the lines around her mouth. "I never told your mother either. She was too afraid to hear it." Her voice quieted. "But you are not afraid, are you, Ivy?"

Fear was not the right word for the knot twisting in Ivy's stomach. She was not sure what to call it. Perhaps dread, perhaps longing. She shook her head, deciding it was safer not to claim bravery, only willingness. "I'm ready," she said, even if her heart pounded unevenly.

Cassandra placed a hand on Ivy's shoulder. "Then come with me."

They climbed the narrow staircase to the attic, their steps echoing on the old wooden boards. Ivy recalled how she had rarely ventured this high in Cassandra's home. There was always a sense of quiet in the upper floors, as if the usual bustle of the city did not dare invade. At the top of the landing, Cassandra stopped at a closed door. A padlock, small but stubborn, guarded the entrance.

"This has been locked for a long time," Cassandra said quietly. She fished a tiny key from her pocket, inserted it, and twisted. The click of metal sounded final. She pushed the door open, revealing a space that smelled of dust and memories.

Ivy took a tentative step inside. The attic's ceiling slanted, exposing wooden beams overhead. Shelves lined the walls, overflowing with musty tomes, jars of dried herbs, half-burned candles, and tarnished relics. The muted glow of a single overhead light gave everything a washed-out sepia tone. She felt like she had entered a hidden library of ghosts.

Cassandra crossed to a large trunk near the far corner. "We kept these items sealed because they bring echoes." She rested her palm on the trunk's lid as though preparing to handle an unpredictable animal. "There are things I never told your mother. Things she was too afraid to remember." She closed her eyes for a moment, gathering resolve, then lifted the lid.

Inside, an assortment of curiosities came into view, small icons carved from dark wood, lengths of braided silk, and a few blood-spattered pages pressed flat between sheets of glass. The metallic tang that rose from them made Ivy's stomach turn. She impressed her fingertips against her temples, fighting off the wave of disquiet. She did not want to imagine what curses or violent rituals those markings hinted at.

"These are tokens from a time when we believed we could speak the right words and change fate," Cassandra murmured. She paused to withdraw a narrow envelope, its edges rusted with age. She turned it over, then set it aside. "It did not go as we hoped."

Ivy pushed a dusty length of cloth aside and discovered a carved bone medallion. Its grooves were filled with dried crimson that could only be old blood. She suppressed a shudder and raised her eyes to Cassandra. "Why would you keep these?" she asked, her voice trembling.

Cassandra set the envelope down. "Because we may need them one day to understand what truly happened." She cleared her throat, then reached deeper into the trunk. "And we may need to do better this time."

At last, Cassandra lifted a rectangular object, wrapped in linen. Ivy caught a flash of reflective gleam through the thin fabric. She realized it was a mirror, longer than she had expected, with a delicate frame that glinted beneath the dusty cloth.

Cassandra braced it on the trunk's edge. The outline looked like a narrow, vintage mirror that one might lean against a wall. Part of the glass had clearly fractured. The cloth sagged in the middle, revealing a jagged line.

"This is her mirror," Cassandra said softly, her voice rough. "Your grandmother's. I do not know every secret it holds, only that she used it to see things beyond ordinary sight."

A memory played in Ivy's mind, foolish childhood rumors of haunted mirrors, ghostly shapes in reflective surfaces. She inhaled through her nose, bracing herself. "You said it has echoes?"

Cassandra nodded and tugged away the linen. The cloth fell, revealing pale shards spiderwebbed across the glass. One large fracture ran from the upper corner to the opposite lower edge. The mirror was set in a tarnished silver frame etched with patterns that reminded Ivy of creeping vines. How anyone had allowed it to remain in such a state was difficult to understand. It looked dangerously close to falling apart.

Ivy's pulse lurched. She stepped forward, slowly leaning in. The moment she met the reflection, her breath froze. There, in the broken shards, she did not see only her own face. The surface shimmered suddenly, as though lit from within by moonlight. Then the image faltered. Something else seemed to stir behind the sheen, behind the cracks. Ivy glimpsed a silhouette that did not match her own. The figure in the mirror was taller, older, and wrapped in the shift of a dark overcoat. Night water poured around that silhouette, like a torrential downpour raining inside the mirror.

She fought the instinct to recoil and forced herself to look deeper. The silhouette shifted again, revealing a woman with hair pinned up tightly, her face austere yet striking. Ivy's heart pounded. An inexplicable recognition tugged at her. She parted her lips, uncertain whether to speak. Rain pelted the scene in the mirror as if it belonged to a different reality. The woman wore an expression that blended urgency with sorrow. Then she spoke, though no sound reached Ivy's ears. Her mouth formed Ivy's name.

Ivy's knees nearly buckled. She gripped the trunk for support. "That's her, isn't it?" she whispered. "My grandmother."

Cassandra moved behind Ivy, her presence a steady pillar of reassurance. "Yes," she answered quietly. She touched Ivy's shoulder. "Her name was Mirella Vale. She was gifted, perhaps more than all of us. And she suffered for it."

The image blurred, as if the rain had grown heavier. Ivy's eyes stung. "She's whispering," she managed. "I can't hear it."

Cassandra nodded. "She left us a message," she said, her voice quiet. "But we were too scared to hear it." She shifted her hand onto Ivy's back, encouraging her to lean closer. "Do you see how the storm churns around her? It is not a memory alone. It is something she tried to send forward, a warning that never arrived."

Ivy pressed a shaking hand to the edge of the mirror and felt a sudden chill radiate from the fractures. The reflection of her grandmother continued mouthing silent words. The corners of the woman's eyes glistened with a grief that echoed across the broken glass. Ivy caught only the shape of her lips forming an incomplete plea. Her chest pinched. She tried not to blink, convinced that the ghostly vision would vanish if she looked away even once.

"What happened to her?" Ivy whispered, her voice unsteady.

Cassandra hesitated, her arms crossing protectively over her chest. "She was caught in a ritual that was meant to protect us all," she said at last. "I only know fragments.

I was too young. But the energies they summoned did not respond the way they intended. She was lost in the aftermath. Some say she drowned, others say the illusions claimed her mind. I do know that one day she was gone. That was the end of everything we believed at the time."

A tear crept down Ivy's cheek. She did not try to wipe it away. The image of her grandmother refused to fade, though the storm roiled more fiercely. It was as if the memory inside the mirror was fighting to remain. "She looks like she is in pain," Ivy said, pressing her other hand against her heart. "Why would she appear now?"

Cassandra exhaled. "Because you are the one who can finally see her. I have tried, but it only gave me nightmares. Your mother never dared look." She paused, her gaze hooded with regret. "Perhaps it always had to be you, Ivy. You stand at the intersection of all we have hidden. My mother's legacy, your father's quiet acceptance, your own gifts, you are the crossing point."

The overhead light wavered, casting the attic in deeper shadows. Ivy steadied her breath and refocused on the vision. Grandmother Mirella seemed close enough to touch, yet she remained unreachable behind the rifts in the glass. The rain roared and circled around her, conjuring the smell of wet earth and electric tension in Ivy's mind, even though the attic air was stale and tinged with dust.

"I can't hear her words," Ivy repeated, leaning her forehead closer to the mirror. She willed her own reflection to fade, wanting only to capture the shape of Mirella's plea. Her grandmother's mouth kept forming desperate syllables that looked almost like a name, Ivy's name or something else. No sound reached her ears.

"She is calling across a veil of time," Cassandra said. "One we cannot simply pierce with a question." She smoothed her palm along the side of the cracked frame, her eyes distant. "The message might not be direct."

Ivy's pulse fluttered as she realized that parts of the mirror's silver backing were etched with faint runes. She studied them through the largest fracture until dizziness threatened to unseat her. "It's alive," she murmured. "This mirror feels alive with memories."

Cassandra draped an arm around Ivy, guiding her gently away. "Careful," she said. "Whatever power remains here is not tamed. That was your grandmother's greatest lesson, that these forces carry a price if we handle them carelessly."

Ivy's lips felt cold, but she forced herself to speak. "You said you were scared. Do you regret not opening this sooner?" Her words trembled. "Maybe if you had, we could have understood more about what's happening to seers in the city, about all the illusions and breakages?"

Cassandra's fingertips tightened on Ivy's shoulder. "I do regret it. But fear once ruled me, Ivy. Fear that she left behind something too big for any of us to bear." She turned her gaze onto the bloodied pages that lay in the trunk. "I was not ready to confront images of what we lost. Perhaps you can be."

For a long moment, neither spoke. The broken mirror reflected Ivy's wide eyes, shimmering with a faint bluish glow. She wanted to ask so many questions. Did this relic tie to the chaos in the Sanctuary? Was this a direct link to the illusions plaguing other seers? Could it reveal how to quiet the roaring tension in her mind that still flared at unpredictable hours?

Yet all she could do was reach for Cassandra's free hand and cling to it. The older woman squeezed back. In the reflection, Mirella's silhouette receded deeper into the storm, as if drifting away in a tide of rain.

Ivy's breath caught. "We can't let her vanish," she said, voice raw. "If she is trying to show us something…"

"I know," Cassandra said, her chest rising and falling with suppressed emotion. "We will not let her vanish, Ivy. But we must tread carefully."

The woman in the mirror hovered as if suspended in a downpour. Ivy felt certain that beyond those sheets of rain lay an entire story left unwritten. She pressed her trembling fingertips onto the largest crack in the glass. A cold shock surged through her hand. The image brightened suddenly, revealing Mirella's mouth shaping an urgent command. The words still came silent, muffled by years of secrecy and fear.

"What do you want from me?" Ivy tried again. "Speak," she murmured, though her voice quivered with tears. "Tell me."

No sound emerged from the mirror. Slowly, the downpour dulled, leaving a pale afterimage. Mirella's form became a faint tracery of light, and then she was gone. Only Ivy's reflection, broken into pieces by the fractured glass, remained.

She swallowed hard, feeling as though she had lost

someone dear all over again. "She was trying to reach out," she managed, her voice ragged.

Cassandra nodded and gently cradled Ivy's shoulders. "She never stopped, I think. She left us a message." Her features looked drawn with sorrow. "But we were too scared to hear it." She gestured to the shattered mirror, then to the trunk of relics. "We kept it here, locked away, believing that if we never looked, it could not hurt us again."

Ivy's hands shook as she drew them to her sides. The fogginess in her head pulsed, yet she resisted the urge to flee. She wanted to know, no matter how unsettling it was. "That message, is it still here?"

Cassandra wore a pensive frown. "I have no doubt," she said. "Mirrors hold echoes of what we hide, intentionally or not. If Mirella put something inside this one, it remains until we fully confront it."

Ivy leaned over the trunk, listening to her own ragged breathing. Outside, the old boards of the house groaned under a shifting breeze. The single light overhead blinked again, threatening to drop them into darkness. In the silence, the reflection in the battered mirror seemed to pulse like a heartbeat.

Ivy's voice dropped to a whisper that felt too loud in the quiet attic. "I think it's still waiting." Cassandra tilted the glass toward the dusty window, letting a sliver of moonlight catch on the shards. Faint runes shimmered between the cracks, rearranging themselves as though waiting for the right eyes. Ivy leaned in, catching a single phrase before it blurred again. *Those who watch must never intervene.*

A chill raced across her skin. "Is that about the people who warned me?" she asked.

"Perhaps," Cassandra whispered. "Your grandmother feared them, yet she trusted their prophecies." The words lingered in Ivy's mind as the runes faded from view, leaving only her fragmented reflection staring back.

CHAPTER

TWELVE

THE WATCHERS

Ivy sensed Ethan's unease the moment he stepped into her shop. He shut the door behind him quietly, and the faint ring of the overhead bell died at once. The sunlight that usually brightened the front display windows felt subdued today, as though something in the air had scraped the brightness from the glass.

She stood behind the wooden counter, organizing a new set of candles, and watched him closely. His shoulders were stiff. He clutched the strap of his worn leather messenger bag, the same way he did whenever he expected trouble.

"Everything okay?" Ivy asked, winding a ribbon around the last candle. Her voice came out soft, yet the tension between them felt electric.

He ran a hand through his hair, leaving it more rumpled than before. "I think someone's following me."

A chill traced along her arms. She set the candle aside

and came around the counter, laying a hand on his forearm. "Ethan, start from the beginning." She felt the rapid beat of his pulse beneath her fingers, and she pressed gently, trying to calm the frantic rhythm.

"I left the Mission earlier this afternoon," he said, stone-faced. "I needed to confirm some details for a piece I'm finishing. As I was walking back to my car, I noticed footsteps behind me. At first, I thought it was just people heading the same way, but the sound stopped whenever I stopped. I turned around more than once, but there was no one there." His gaze moved to the front window, as though he expected to see a reflection lurking in the street. "It was weird. One time, I caught a shape in the corner of my eye. Then it was gone."

Ivy studied him, worry rising. "You're sure it wasn't a coincidence?"

He shook his head. "I trust my instincts. Something was off."

She released his arm and brushed a stray curl away from her cheek. The uncertainty between them carried overlapping questions they were too uneasy to voice. Who would follow Ethan, and why? She half-expected the name Lucien to rise in her mind, but something told her this was a different kind of threat.

Before she could ask again, Robin pushed open the shop's back door, a small package of new tarot decks in her arms. She set it down on a stool. "Hey, you two look like someone died. What am I missing?"

Ivy removed her hand from Ethan's arm, wordless. She

glanced at him, and he let out a slow breath. His mouth tightened, but he turned to Robin.

"We think someone's trailing me," he said, his voice low. "Hiding every time I try to look."

Robin's brows shot up. Her eyes moved to Ivy, then to Ethan, as if searching for an immediate explanation. "That's unnerving."

Ethan nodded. "I was ready to forget it and keep going, but something pulled me into an alley near Kearny Street. I swore I saw a shape in the glass reflection across a boarded window."

"Did you check?" Ivy asked, her pulse fluttering.

"Yeah, but it vanished. Like a shadow. When I drove here, I took a longer route just to see if I was being tailed, but if they were behind me, they knew how to stay hidden. When I turned the final time," Ethan continued, "I swear I saw the edge of a dark cloak disappearing around the corner. It had this mark, an eye enclosed in a broken circle. The same emblem that man at the vigil wore."

Ivy's pulse skipped. She remembered the dying stranger's warning and the way his sleeve had brushed her wrist, revealing that sigil. "You think it's connected?" she whispered.

"I do," Ethan said. "Whoever they are, they want us wary but won't step out of the shadows."

A silence fell, and Ivy noticed how her heart had begun to hammer. She wondered whether to mention the times she, too, had felt eyes on her in recent weeks. Vestiges of the Sanctuary? Or another group entirely?

Robin set a reassuring hand on Ethan's shoulder. "Let's not stand here in dread. Is there anything else?"

Ethan exhaled, as though unburdening part of his fear. "There is." He paused. "After the alley, I went searching in that area. I was compelled to keep looking around Kearny, to catch whoever this was. That's when I found a book-store that isn't on any map or listing I've ever seen." He paused, noticing Ivy's uncertain frown. "It doesn't have a name or a sign out front. The door was unlocked. No clerk. No sign of activity."

Ivy sensed a coil of apprehension in her gut. "But someone must own it."

He lifted a hand in a vague gesture. "I have no idea. I only know that I let myself in. Rows of strange tomes, half of them in languages I can't read. I was drawn to one shelf in particular. And I found this."

He unzipped his bag and withdrew a dusty volume bound in deep red leather. Gold filigree lined its edges, though the designs were half-obscured by smudges. He held it out to Ivy.

She gazed at it warily. A faint tingle moved across her skin. "The Seer's Reckoning," she read from the gilded title. A pang of recognition tugged at her, though she had never seen the book before. She traced a fingertip along the worn spine.

"It had your name on the inside cover," Ethan murmured, his voice tight. "In neat, old-fashioned cursive. The page is dated decades ago."

Her chest constricted. "That can't be possible."

He opened the book to a front page with an ex-libris stamp, a stylized outline of an eye, ringed by a half circle of smaller glyphs. Below that, in graceful handwriting, was her first and last name: Ivy Maren Lewis.

Robin glanced over Ivy's shoulder. "What in the world?"

Ivy's vision swam. She tried to quell the fluttery panic in her stomach. "We should let Cassandra see this," she said, her voice betraying more confidence than she felt. "She might know what this symbol means, or why my name is here. She's encountered a lot of old seer texts."

She looked at Ethan and saw relief spread across his features. He wanted answers as much as she did.

Robin passed them a set of keys from the counter. "Go. I can handle the shop until closing. Just text me if you need backup."

Ivy nodded, still clutching the book under one arm. "Thank you." She turned to Ethan. "Let's see if Cassandra is at home."

They rode in Ethan's car. The early evening light tinted San Francisco's sky with muted grays. Fog clung to the taller buildings, drifting like a restless spirit. Ivy kept glancing in the side mirrors, her chest tightened by a constant suspicion that someone lurked behind them. Ethan fiddled with the radio absentmindedly, but left it off after static filled the speakers. They barely spoke. Each time she looked at the book in her lap, her skin pricked, as though it carried its own silent heartbeat.

At Cassandra's Nob Hill townhouse, Ivy felt a surge of

that same dreadful awareness. She saw no watchers on the street. No silhouettes in the windows. Yet the quiet that pressed in around them felt unnaturally heavy. She shared a tense look with Ethan before knocking.

Cassandra answered almost immediately, wearing a long black tunic. Her hair was pulled back from her sharp face, and worry lined her brow. Without a word, she beckoned them inside.

The townhouse's interior smelled of warmed cloves and burnt sage. Candles pulsed in small glass cups along the mantel, reflecting pinpricks of light across the mirrored frames and old family photos. Ivy tried not to stare at the large antique mirror half-draped in cloth on the far wall. She breathed in through her nose, trying to steady herself.

Cassandra ushered them to the living room. She gestured toward a low table, inviting them to sit. Ivy and Ethan took seats on the velvet settee, and Ivy placed the book on the table with both hands.

"We found this," she said softly. "Or more accurately, Ethan found it. My name is written just inside the cover."

Cassandra's expression froze. She hesitated, then picked up the volume gingerly. Her gaze moved over the filigree, then the spine, then the first page. Ivy watched her aunt's shoulders tense. A shallow breath escaped Cassandra.

"The Seer's Reckoning," Cassandra whispered. "It is rumored to carry records of cataclysmic visions. Some mention was made of it in my mother's journals. But I never actually saw a copy until now." She turned to the page with Ivy's name. "This makes no sense. This signature…"

Ivy's throat felt tight. She waited, but Cassandra seemed unwilling to finish the thought. Instead, her aunt's face went pale, ghostly white. She set the book down, then pressed her fingertips against her temple, as though warding off a migraine.

Ethan shifted on the settee. "Do you know why it would list Ivy's name? Or who might have placed it in that hidden bookstore?"

Cassandra closed her eyes. "They are testing boundaries," she said, her voice taut. "Not just hers, but yours." She let the words hang in the air, each syllable weighted with foreboding. Then she lifted her gaze to Ethan. "If this was left for you to find, it means whomever followed you wanted you to deliver it to Ivy. Or to me."

Ethan glanced from the book to Ivy. "The stalker who led me there might be one of them," he said.

"A Watcher." Cassandra looked troubled. "If so, they want us to prepare for whatever storm they foresee. But they will never stand beside us." The realization left Ivy uneasy. Somewhere beyond the safety of Cassandra's parlor, those silent observers moved unseen, recording her every step.

"Watchers," Ethan repeated softly. "The man from the vigil used that term before he died."

Cassandra nodded. "They believe in observing potential catastrophes and documenting them, nothing more. Interference is forbidden." She tapped the cover of the book. "Leaving this for you was their version of a warning."

Ivy frowned at the crimson volume. "So they want us cautious, but they won't help?"

"Exactly," Cassandra said. "They see themselves as guardians of prophecy. They try to steer seers without ever intervening directly."

THIRTEEN

THE EMPATH'S WARNING

Ivy braced herself against a gust of wind as she stepped off the curb, squinting through the late-afternoon light. Traffic wove past, and the air smelled faintly of fried dough and roasted coffee beans. She exhaled slowly, trying to steady the vibration lingering under her skin. The last few nights had offered her little rest, only flashes of restless half-visions.

Robin had invited her to a pop-up reading event in a converted warehouse near *The Mission*. Unofficially, it was a gathering of indie artists, spiritual readers, and curious locals looking for novelty. Officially, it was an evening of bric-a-brac, rummaged items, and a horde of tarot enthusiasts who wanted their fortunes read by candlelight. Ivy took another breath and walked toward the wide doors propped open by two large crates. The faint music of a live violin drifted out, mixing with the murmur of voices inside.

She found Robin near a collapsible table, shuffling a

deck of luminous cards that caught every glint of overhead light. Strings of fairy lights crossed the high ceilings, giving the interior a playful glow. Robin flashed her a grin as soon as they noticed her approach.

"Finally," Robin teased. "I thought you had bailed."

"I nearly did," Ivy admitted. She glanced around the brick-walled space, noticing small clusters of people browsing cassette tapes, thrift clothes, or handcrafted jewelry. Vendors had arranged their makeshift booths in a sprawling semicircle, leaving the center of the warehouse open for foot traffic. "Work took longer than I planned."

Robin's brows lifted. "Work," she repeated wryly, clearly referencing the tension that had become Ivy's new normal, half mundane tasks at her shop, half worn attempts to navigate her so-called gift. "Glad you made it, though. I have someone for you to meet."

Ivy followed Robin's gaze to a short figure standing near a folding chair draped with a patchwork blanket. He wore a soft, oversized cardigan and clutched a small locket in one hand. A sign perched on a stool next to them read *Rowan Vega, Empathic Readings*. Rowan's eyes were downcast, as if worried about making contact with passersby. Ivy felt a pang of recognition. She knew the kind of self-conscious posture that came with having a power you never asked for.

Robin bobbed her head in Rowan's direction. "He's a friend," Robin said quietly. "I mentioned you a while back, asked if he had suggestions for taming runaway visions. He doesn't see the future, but he sees color. Emotions in color. And believe me, he's real."

Ivy nodded, curiosity rising. "He must be exhausted in a crowd like this."

"He is," Robin replied, lips tightening with concern. "That's why I keep an eye on him. Come on."

They wove through clusters of onlookers flipping through crystal pendants and old vinyls. Somewhere in the corner, someone rang a small gong, prompting a few startled gasps. Ivy noticed Ethan standing near a table of vintage postcards, arms crossed as he pretended to examine them. He caught her glance and offered a half-smile that didn't quite reach his eyes. Though she and Ethan had found some semblance of fragile understanding, especially after he had seen enough of her abilities to believe, she sensed that new doubts had begun gnawing at him again. He looked tense, and the set of his jaw made her want to reach out, but she let him be for the moment. For once, she wanted to greet someone without the weight of an argument on her shoulders.

When they reached Rowan, Robin introduced them with a reassuring pat to Rowan's shoulder. Rowan looked up, revealing soft features and warm brown eyes that seemed simultaneously curious and shy.

"Ivy," Robin said, "this is Rowan. Rowan, this is Ivy."

Rowan smiled with trembling earnestness. "Nice to meet you." His voice came out subdued, barely above the hum of conversation around them.

"You too," Ivy said gently. "Robin's told me a little about your abilities."

Rowan's cheeks warmed. "That's kind of her. I'm not as well-known as the tarot readers here."

Robin snorted. "That's because you're new in town. But trust me, you'll get a following fast."

Rowan nodded, then looked at Ivy again. It was a look that felt almost searching, as though Rowan reached for something unseen. Ivy's stomach dipped with apprehension. She had experienced scrutiny from other seers before, but those encounters were usually laced with unspoken agendas or cryptic riddles. Rowan's gaze felt different, open, hesitant, yet impossibly perceptive.

"Do you mind if I?" Rowan pointed to Ivy's hand. "Empaths usually have some line we shouldn't cross without permission, but a handshake is enough for me to sense the surface."

Ivy swallowed. "It's okay. Go ahead."

She offered her hand, and Rowan took it, his fingertips barely curling around Ivy's. The contact sent a tiny ripple of awareness up Ivy's arm. She couldn't quite describe it, almost like static electricity in the air between them. She held her breath.

Rowan's eyes widened, and he sucked in a sharp, startled gulp of air. His grip trembled. "You're leaking red," he murmured, his voice hollow with surprise. "Grief. Regret. But not all yours."

Ivy felt her chest squeeze. She wasn't sure what she feared more, that Rowan was right or that she'd end up sobbing right here among the folding tables. "Not all mine?" she repeated, trying to keep her tone neutral.

Rowan's eyes drifted closed, as if focusing on a kaleidoscope only he could see. A moment later, his head tilted. "No. The color is layered around you, but it's not rooted in you. It's coming from a man, I think." He paused, brows knitting in concentration. "He has one foot in your world, one in his own. That's how it feels."

Ivy suppressed a shiver. Her thoughts darted to Lucien for one lingering second, then to Ethan. Both men were in her life, each in such different ways that she frequently felt tugged in two directions. "Any sense of who? Or how?" she asked quietly.

Rowan opened his eyes and released Ivy's hand with a shaky breath. "It's not clear," he apologized, his voice trembling with sincerity. "But that shade of red usually suggests unspoken conflict, a push and pull between guilt and longing. It bleeds into you. Leaves its mark."

For a moment, Ivy said nothing. She struggled to swallow around a sudden dryness in her throat. If Rowan saw any hint of regret, it could easily belong to Lucien and the complicated secrets they shared. Or maybe it belonged to Ethan, who had grown more and more uneasy as Ivy delved deeper into the Sanctuary's world. Either way, Ivy recognized how guilt could seep into every conversation, every glance. It weighed on her like an invisible chain.

Robin touched Rowan's arm, concern etched across their features. "You okay?" she asked, her voice gentle.

Rowan nodded, though he still looked frazzled. "Yeah, just a lot of color. Ivy's aura is intense. I guess because so many feelings feed into it."

Ivy exhaled a soft laugh. "That's one way to put it."

Before any of them could speak again, Ethan slid up beside Ivy, offering a clipped nod to Rowan and Robin.

"Hey," he said, sliding his hands into his jacket pockets. "Everything all right over here?"

Robin put on a bright smile. "We're good. Rowan just gave Ivy a bit of empathic insight."

Ethan didn't look amused. "Insight, huh?" he repeated. His skepticism was less overt than usual, but Ivy caught the tension in his tone. He glanced around as though checking if anyone might overhear. Then his attention settled on Ivy, his lower voice betraying his worry. "We need to talk privately. Now."

Robin arched an eyebrow but made no comment. Rowan stepped back, clearly uncomfortable. Ivy studied Ethan's rigid posture, noticing the faint shadows under his eyes. She had no idea what he had discovered or what had fueled this urgency, but her gut told her it revolved around his mounting suspicion of the Sanctuary.

She turned to Robin. "I'll be back in a minute," she said softly, offering Rowan an apologetic smile. Rowan nodded without protest, already closing himself off from the surge of energy that seemed to press in from every corner of the warehouse.

Ethan led her past a row of vendors selling homemade soaps and beeswax candles, until they reached a far corner of the space where empty crates were stacked. The low hum of a needle hitting vinyl drifted from a DJ booth across the room. Soft conversation continued in the distance, but they had enough privacy to speak freely.

"What's going on?" Ivy asked, crossing her arms to steel herself for whatever he was about to say.

He ran a hand through his hair, his eyes lighting with

worry. "I've been digging," he said, his voice tight. "I have some contacts, people who keep tabs on odd happenings in the city. One of them told me that the Sanctuary has deeper ties than we thought. They're not just a safe haven for seers. They have a history of, well..." He trailed off, searching for the right words. "Exploiting people who are powerful. Recruiting them in secret. Sometimes it starts innocent, but it doesn't always stay that way."

Ivy's stomach twisted. She remembered scraps of rumors, glimpses of half-told warnings about the old Circle. And yes, she had felt the undercurrent of caution around Lucien. "You're talking about manipulative practices," she summarized. "You think they brought me in just to take advantage of my abilities."

Ethan's gaze was sure and unyielding. "Yes, exactly that. Look, everything you've told me about Lucien, about the Marking, the glyph, the group sessions, none of it sounds safe. You're trusting them, but you don't really know their endgame."

Ivy's jaw tightened at the mention of Lucien's name. She had tried to shift her thoughts away from him, especially after the last time he'd shown up uninvited at her door. The reminder unsettled her more than she cared to admit. "They're not all Lucien," she said quietly. "There are others who genuinely seem to want knowledge, not power."

He took a step closer, his voice low. "You told me you feel their energy pulsing through you sometimes, that you can't always tell where your feelings end and theirs begin. That isn't normal, Ivy. That's dangerous. You rely on them for answers, but they might be the ones twisting your visions in the first place."

An urge to defend the Sanctuary rose inside her. She thought of Selene's quiet vulnerability in front of mirrors, of Cassian's soft sketches brimming with unanswered questions, of Thalia who had offered gentle solidarity when Ivy shared her struggles. Were they all part of some grand conspiracy? Or were they, like Ivy, hurting, searching for stability in a world that ridiculed what they could do?

"They've helped me understand my gift," she countered, her voice rising. Several heads turned in their direction, but she kept going. "They're the ones who told me I wasn't crazy, that I wasn't alone."

Ethan pressed his lips together, glancing away. "I know," he said at last. "I understand why you feel loyal to them. But you have to consider the possibility that they're using you. Look at everything you've been through. If these people truly respected your freedom, they wouldn't let you get tangled in secrets and cryptic half-answers."

Ivy's heart pounded, torn between frustration and the gnawing sense that the Sanctuary, for all its weirdness, had welcomed her in ways no one else had. She remembered how lonely she'd felt when the media pinned her as "The BART Oracle," how cut off she was from her own parents, who never truly believed in her. Then the Sanctuary had appeared with open arms, letting her unlock abilities she barely understood.

Her pulse thundered. She couldn't deny Ethan's points. She had suspected manipulations too, especially from Lucien, with his smoldering eyes and riddles. Yet she also remembered Rowan's words. "You're leaking red. A man with one foot in your world." She shivered at the memory, uncertain who that man might be in the end.

Ethan searched her face. "I'm not telling you to cut all ties," he said. "I just want you to be safe. And I'm worried you're trusting the wrong people. Or the wrong man."

She bit her lip, refusing to let tears form. "If the Sanctuary lets me fully explore my gift, maybe that's worth the risk. At least they're not afraid of me."

"Who says they're not afraid?" Ethan cut in. "Fear is at the root of half the things they do. You told me they're terrified of some big meltdown if your power goes unchecked. They're all edgy around you."

She shook her head, stepping away from the crates. "What if..." She wrestled the words out, uncertain if she believed them or if she only wanted to. "What if they're the only ones not afraid of me?"

A brittle silence hung between them. Time seemed to slow, the pop-up event's background noise fading like a distant tide. Ivy could see the hint of pain in Ethan's eyes, but she could no longer squash the question pressing at her chest. Because whatever his motives, Lucien had never once flinched at her raw power. And neither had Thalia, Cassian, or Selene.

Her whisper lingered in the air, echoing with a fervor that both frightened and emboldened her.

"What if they're the only ones not afraid of me?"

FOURTEEN

THE BINDING THREAD

Ivy inhaled slowly as she stepped across the threshold of the hidden chamber beneath the Sanctuary. A single lantern lit the rough stone passage, and its dim, wavering glow multiplied the shadows dancing against the walls. The cavernous space ahead pulsed with a heavy silence, like a living heartbeat buried deep in the earth.

Lucien had extended his invitation earlier that morning through a messenger who arrived at Ivy's apartment just after sunrise. The envelope contained only a single line of graceful handwriting that read, *Tonight, you will see how we shape possibility. Come alone.* She felt both wariness and curiosity at those words, and although a coil of dread tightened in her stomach at the thought of facing Lucien again, she decided to attend. The circle's warnings and whispers had grown darker over the past weeks. If she wished to understand her own role within this crumbling society of seers, she would need to see their rituals up close.

At the end of the hallway, a heavy wooden door stood ajar, and the sound of conversation drifted out. Ivy paused, resting her palm against the cold doorframe. The pressure in the air reminded her of a thunderstorm about to break, as though hidden currents whirled just beyond view.

She pushed the door open. Candlelight wavered in every direction, rising from tall iron candelabras arranged in a ring around a wide circular chamber. The ceiling curved overhead, riddled with drips of condensation that gleamed in the glow. About a dozen figures had gathered around a low stone platform at the center. Some were seated on carved wooden chairs, while others stood or knelt on threadbare rugs.

Selene, the mirror-scrying seer with translucent skin, was there. She glanced up at Ivy's entrance and inclined her head in the barest of greetings. A few other faces turned her way, their expressions cautious or curious. Cassian, the silent teenage boy, sat on the floor with a leather-bound sketchbook propped against his knees. His pencil scratched lightly across a page, and he did not pause to greet Ivy. Beside him, Thalia offered Ivy a polite nod. Everyone seemed tense, as though bracing for something they did not fully understand.

Then Lucien stepped forward from within the candlelit ring. He wore a long black coat, and his pale eyes glowed with muted intensity in the warm light. He lifted a hand in welcome. "Ivy," he said, his voice smooth and commanding. "You came."

She nodded, stepping farther into the room until she

stood between the chairs and the ring of candles. "I did," she said. Her pulse thrummed in her temples. She tried not to stare at his face for too long, afraid of the pull that always tugged at her whenever he fixed his attention on her. "Though I am still not certain what you expect me to see."

Lucien smiled faintly. "Tonight's ritual is called the Binding Thread. Each of us will contribute a strand of ourselves, literal and psychic, into a woven pattern meant to foretell convergence. The circle has used this practice for generations when a turning point looms before us."

Selene moved to stand at Lucien's side, her black hair catching the candlelight. She kept her gaze focused on the floor. At her feet lay a coil of pale thread, so thin and delicate that it resembled a spider's silk. Ivy noticed more coils like it placed around the circle. She guessed they belonged to the others, each spool representing a link from its owner.

"Are you ready?" Lucien asked softly. His voice held a gentle note, but Ivy sensed steel beneath it, the unwavering confidence that he alone directed and understood this ritual's outcome.

She swallowed, glancing around the room. Each person there seemed somberly expectant. Their unspoken message was clear. This ceremony mattered. Any hesitation might be seen as betrayal or fear. Gathering her resolve, Ivy stepped closer to the stone platform. "I am," she managed.

Lucien gestured to those assembled. "Then let us begin. To start, each one of us will lay our thread along the weaving frame and focus on what we sense of the future. When the pattern forms, we will see if our separate visions converge or diverge."

He moved toward the center, where a circular wooden stand rose from the stone. It resembled a shallow loom, pinned with tiny hooks around the rim. Lucien took a spool of dark gray thread from within his coat and touched it to his lips. For a moment, he closed his eyes. The air in the room crackled. Then he placed the end of his thread around a hook, pulling it taut across the loom until the spool was nearly empty. He passed its length carefully, hooking it in a gentle spiral across the center. As he did, the candles seemed to spark a little brighter.

When Lucien finished, he nodded at Selene. She stepped forward with her spool of pale thread, placed one end against a hook beside Lucien's, and began weaving the new line across his. The tension in the air rose with each careful motion. Her expression turned distant, as if she saw images flitting before her. She wove quickly, binding pale thread around the darker lines Lucien had laid. A faint shimmer rose from the loom, like heat waves dancing above pavement.

One after another, the other seers approached. Thalia's spool was a muted sage-green, adding a steady, earthy quality to the emerging pattern. Cassian's thread was almost colorless, though Ivy swore she saw faint gold flecks in the fibers whenever the boy's pencil paused and his eyes darted over to watch her. The hum at the center of the chamber grew stronger, resonating through Ivy's chest.

As more threads were woven, the lines on the loom took on the shape of a growing web. Hints of luminous energy blinked around its strands. Ivy noticed that every seer wore a look of deep introspection while weaving, as though each was seeing some private vision. From time to time, one would pause, draw a breath, and then continue, as though processing a sudden jolt of insight or fear.

Finally, Lucien turned to Ivy and extended a hand. A spool of thread rested in his palm, unspun and waiting. She stared at it, noticing immediately how different it looked from the others. Its color was difficult to name, shifting between silver and a darker hue that edged toward midnight blue. The spool felt almost warm in her hand. Ivy's breathing turned shallow. She tried to calm her pulse, but anticipation coiled in her belly.

"Your turn," Lucien said gently. His gaze slipped across her features. "It is time to reveal your piece in this tapestry."

Ivy swallowed again, stepping to the loom's edge. Uncertainty gnawed at her. She recognized the potential of this moment. She remembered the times she had touched mirrors or runes, only to have images explode into her mind. This spool felt even more potent. She placed the free end at a hook near the top of the loom and began weaving slowly, mindful not to pull too hard. Each pass of her thread slid across the others, linking them all. With each breath, her senses sharpened, and she felt the whisper of unspoken messages in the air.

Halfway through her weaving, she sensed a shift. It was subtle at first, a slight tremor that rattled the loom's wooden frame. Lucien's fingers stirred at the corner of her vision, but he said nothing. Then the tremor grew stronger, and Ivy froze. The thread in her hand quivered as if it had a pulse. She tried to place it around the next hook, but the strands on the loom pulled taut, resisting her motion. Her heart thudded uncomfortably fast.

She forced the spool forward and looped the strand into the hooks, ignoring the prickling along her arms. The moment she secured it, the entire weaving shuddered. Light sparked, flaring bright as lightning against the stone walls. The air in the chamber seemed to recede into a sudden quiet. Ivy stepped back, her chest clenched.

Threads violently knotted before her eyes, twisting together as though possessed by an unseen hand. A tangle formed in the center, more chaotic than any pattern the others had created. Selene let out a sharp breath. Thalia reached out in alarm, but Lucien lifted a hand to stop her from interfering. The weaving jerked again, the lines pulling tight.

Then the knot began to shift into a shape. Ivy blinked, uncertain if her mind was playing a trick on her. Slowly, the twisted threads took on the outline of two overlapping eyes, each pupil split by a flame-like slash. Faint sparks traced the pattern's edges. In the silence that fell, Ivy could only stare. The symbol's presence pulsed like a living heartbeat, raw and disquieting.

"That is not supposed to happen," whispered someone behind her. It might have been Cassian, though the boy generally never spoke. Soft murmurs spread around the room, passing from one seer to the next. Ivy heard quick exclamations. "What does it mean?" "Have you ever seen anything like that?" "Impossible." The wave of voices rose and fell like a panicked tide.

Ivy stepped back another pace. The spool nearly fell from her hands, and she set it on the floor to let her shaking fingers find empty air. Heat coursed along her skin, and an echo of pain throbbed in her temple. She tried to steady her breathing. The sense of being surrounded pressed in from all sides. She felt as if the entire chamber were looking at her, the candles now reduced to a faint haze in her peripheral vision.

Selene's voice, quiet and tremulous, broke through the murmurs. "She is causing the distortion," she said. "She is the unraveling."

Ivy's heart lurched. *Unraveling.* The word hung in the stillness, weighted with fear and awe. It struck her chest like a blow, stirring memories of the subtle warnings offered by Cassandra and Rowan. She had sensed that her presence amplified visions, that she was a conduit for psychic energy. Yet seeing this fracturing shape, the double eye split by flame, in the very center of their most sacred ritual shook her more than she cared to admit.

Lucien's gaze moved to Ivy, then back to the twisted pattern in the loom. His features were unreadable, though a faint tension lined the corners of his mouth. For a moment, he seemed poised to speak. He did not. He turned instead, facing the threads. The silence grew heavier, thick with unasked questions.

Thalia took a cautious step forward, but her voice quivered. "Lucien, can you address this?" She gestured at the knotted shape, her hand trembling. "Whatever has formed is not from our collective intention."

Lucien remained motionless. Ivy could not read him. Alarm crackled like static in the circle of seers, yet he kept his composure. He placed a palm near the tangle of threads without touching them, as if listening for an echo. Then he met Ivy's eyes, and for a heartbeat, she felt the force of his scrutiny. It reminded her of a wave crashing against a shore, relentless and inescapable.

She recognized that no one truly understood what had just happened, not even Lucien. Perhaps that lack of clarity was what shook her most. Their entire assembly had been prepared for a glimpse of the future, yet the future they received was stark, ominous, and confusing. The double eye seemed to accuse her of something she could not name.

Her pulse still pounded. With a shaking breath, she broke Lucien's gaze and stepped out of the loom's circle. "I need to go," she managed weakly. Her heart hammered as she turned and pushed through the small crowd. Someone reached out, but she slipped from their grasp. The chamber's candlelit shadows twisted around her like living specters.

No one tried to stop her when she reached the hall. Perhaps they were too stunned by the pattern's violent shift. Ivy barely saw where she was going. She only knew she had to escape that suffocating space before she gave in to the wave of panic rising in her throat. Somewhere behind her, voices erupted in argument or alarm, but she did not listen. She slipped through the doorway into the damp corridor, her footsteps echoing on stone.

As soon as she found the stairwell that led upward, her breath came in ragged gasps. She braced a hand against the cold wall. Her mind reeled with the image of those knotted threads forming the double eye. Selene's quiet pronouncement echoed in her ears. *She is the unraveling.* Ivy pressed the back of her hand to her mouth, fighting the sting of tears. She had been seeking a place in this world, an understanding of her gifts, but now she felt as though she stood at the heart of something that might destroy everything around her.

She climbed the winding steps, drawn forward by the faint promise of fresher air at the end of the passage. The clang of her heartbeat in her head would not subside. She remembered Lucien's earlier words about shaping possibility. Yet the future she had just witnessed looked less like a promise and more like a broken reflection.

At last, Ivy emerged onto a small upper landing. A lantern revealed the final door out of the Sanctuary's bowels. She shoved it open, stumbling into the cramped bookstore storeroom that concealed the Sanctuary's entrance. A single overhead bulb buzzed, pale and mundane, but the normalcy of that simple electric light felt jarring in the wake of chanting candles and threads gone wild.

Her breath began to steady. She had to keep moving. She crossed the storeroom, navigating past stacked crates of old tomes and hidden relics. The second door led to the main bookstore, and from there, a side exit to Chinatown's nighttime streets. She yearned for the chill of open air and the anonymity of city lights. Anything to escape the pressing certainty that she had triggered something none of them were prepared to face.

She paused just inside the bookstore. A pang of worry for the others spread through her mind. Thalia had looked frightened. Selene had spoken as though naming a prophecy. Cassian had finally spoken, or perhaps that was just another voice in the crowd. And Lucien, she could not decipher him. She imagined the loom behind them, the double eye still glowing at the center. The image brought fresh tremors to her hands.

Swallowing hard, she squared her shoulders. She needed time to process what had happened, to figure out why her thread alone had warped the weaving in such a grim way. Part of her feared that the others would turn on her for destroying, or at least tainting, the ceremony. Another part of her whispered that maybe they would fear her enough to take drastic action. She could not decide which outcome frightened her more.

She stepped outside into the cool air, letting the brisk night breeze wash over her cheeks. Cars rumbled past, and neon signs blinked above the sidewalk. A wave of chatter from passing pedestrians rose and fell without noticing her. The mundane bustle of Chinatown after dark enveloped her in a strange comfort, proving that life carried on, indifferent to the mysteries that lurked below.

Ivy pressed a hand over her heart, inhaling the faint smell of street food and incense. She thought of Ethan, of Cassandra, of Robin. Part of her wanted to find them, to confide in someone who might drown out the echo of Selene's words. Yet a deeper part of her wanted to run, flee into the city's anonymity, and vanish before she could be seen as the harbinger of ruin.

She cleared her throat, taking a final, unsteady breath. The memory of the double eye, haloed by flame, burned behind her eyelids. It blazed like a verdict she did not want. For the first time, she felt a chill that went deeper than simple fear. She realized that she might not only be part of a prophecy or an important thread in someone else's tapestry. She could be the strand that unravels everything.

Shivering, she started walking down the sidewalk, the wind ruffling her hair. The phrases from the gathering echoed in her thoughts, each step carrying her away from the Sanctuary and deeper into the city. She did not look back. Her mind was full of questions, none of which she knew how to answer. All she could do was keep walking, shaken to her core, with one thought resounding in every heartbeat.

She might be the breaking point.

FIFTEEN

FRACTURES IN THE CIRCLE

Ivy stood in the far corner of the Sanctuary's lower hall, watching small clusters of seers drift into murmured conversation. Candles perched on wrought-iron stands sent streaks of pale light across the smooth walls. At other gatherings, she would have felt an undercurrent of shared purpose here, a sense that everyone was pulling threads of the same tapestry to foresee potential futures. Tonight felt different. The hallway hummed with a tension that made her stomach tighten.

She had come because a hastily arranged meeting had been announced to discuss the aftermath of the séance that took place mere hours ago. Headaches, sudden visions, and whispered blame had flourished in its wake. Ivy had not slept since adding her thread to that ill-fated weaving. Each time she closed her eyes, she saw the double eye split by flame, its violent message seared into her mind.

She pressed her hand over the aura glyph on her wrist.

It pulsed in faint, ragged beats that matched the nerves rattling inside her. She had tried to calm it by breathing slowly, counting heartbeats, but the glyph remained restless against her skin. She wondered if the others sensed it as well.

A broad wooden door at the far end of the corridor creaked open. Selene emerged first, her pale face drawn with worry. Her black hair fell in a loose braid down one shoulder. She paused near one of the torches, glancing over the handful of assembled seers. Thalia followed on quick heels. The older woman gave Ivy a nervous half-smile before joining Selene. Cassian, the quiet boy, trailed behind, hugging his sketchbook so tightly it appeared ready to crumble. And then, stepping in last, Lucien moved with cool assurance. He held his chin high, his pale eyes scanning the room. The silence that followed felt as though every ounce of breath had vanished. Members of the Sanctuary closed ranks, forming a loose half-circle around them.

Ivy swallowed when she realized nobody was speaking. Was the entire meeting orchestrated to confront her? A slow burn of dread coiled along the base of her spine. She felt Robin approach from behind, offering a silent, protective presence.

Selene cleared her throat. "Thank you all for gathering on short notice. We have urgent matters to address." She rubbed her neck as if massaging away a knot. "After last night's weaving, some of our members," her dark eyes moved to a small knot of seers leaning against the wall, "are suffering from erratic visions. Others reported increased psychic strain."

Thalia stepped forward, her voice stifled. "And a few are convinced that the weave itself collapsed on a point of instability."

A ripple of movement passed through the listeners. Ivy felt a spike of anxiety. Every gaze seemed to tilt in her direction, whether intentionally or not. The weight of it pressed on her lungs. She reminded herself to breathe, though each inhalation felt shallow.

One of the older seers, a woman named Dara, who specialized in dream reading, fixed Ivy with an uneasy stare. "It was calm before," Dara said, tucking strands of gray hair behind her ears. "The pattern showed a neutral field. The very moment Ivy's strand touched, the net twisted."

Ivy opened her mouth, prepared to defend herself, but Robin's hand against her back urged patience. Lucien stood unmoving. He had not spoken once. His silence cut through her more painfully than if he had directed accusations.

A short figure in a hooded cloak muttered, "We should not jump to blame. There might be external factors. The watchers. Or a resonance we overlooked."

Selene nodded. "True, we should consider everything. But the disruptions are real, and they began with the final thread." Her tone was measured, but her gaze had sharpened.

Ivy's hands trembled. She clenched them into fists at her sides. "I didn't mean for anything to break," she managed, her voice soft. "I simply followed what Lucien asked. We all contributed, but my thread took on that shape. I don't know why."

"It was no ordinary shape." Dara's voice rose, tension filling each syllable. "You saw it. A double eye with a flame-cast line through it. That's an omen none of us has deciphered before."

"It might be a sign," Thalia offered cautiously, though there was worry in her eyes. "Not necessarily an evil one. We have to proceed carefully."

Selene exhaled, turning to Lucien. "You led the rite," she said. "What is your perspective on all this?"

He regarded Selene with the faintest tilt of his head. His face betrayed little. "Symbols are not always immediate in meaning," he said, measured. "It may represent a shift. A prophecy. Or, as Thalia stated, a sign of change." He paused, glancing at Ivy. Something unreadable glinted in his gaze. "More importantly, it shows that the Circle stands at a tender juncture. We cannot ignore the effect this has had."

Ivy waited for him to say more, to declare that the group should support her or at least keep exploring. Instead, he went silent again. The space between them filled with the tension of unspoken charges.

Selene broke into that silence. "We had an emergency meeting of the Sanctuary's core members earlier," she said. "We weighed the evidence, the pattern, the after-shocks." She cleared her throat again. Her eyes darted once more to Ivy. "And we decided that it may be best for Ivy to refrain from attending the next vision gathering."

Ivy felt the words like a slap. She looked from Selene to Lucien, hoping someone would refute the suggestion. No one spoke up. A quiet spread through the watchers.

"It's for your safety," Selene continued. "Our next gathering will be highly charged. If the presence of your thread is amplifying or destabilizing our psychic web, then perhaps we should keep your powers from tangling with ours until we have a better understanding of what caused that anomaly."

Silence pressed on Ivy's ears like an oncoming storm. Thalia lowered her gaze apologetically. Cassian watched her with wide eyes, the tip of his pencil pressing against a blank page. She glimpsed the edge of a half-formed eye drawn there.

Robin could not hold back. "That's ridiculous,"she snapped, stepping forward. Her voice echoed against the stone. "You think cutting Ivy out will fix your problems? She's not some disease you can quarantine."

"Robin," Selene began, her voice trembling, "you have not seen the harm. My mirror fractured last night. Lucien's own weaving is incomplete. We do not fully know how Ivy's conduit ability interacts with every seer here. We must manage risk."

"Manage risk?" Robin scoffed. "Since when do we isolate someone who's just as confused as the rest of you? Did any of you consider actually helping her figure out what that symbol means?"

Thalia placed a gentle hand on Robin's arm. "We want to help. But we must proceed in an orderly way. This is not about accusing Ivy. It is about caution. Give us time to reestablish equilibrium."

Robin shrugged her off, her eyes blazing. Ivy's heart lurched. She was grateful for Robin's loyalty, but she also felt exhausted by the fight. She could sense the group's combined fear pressing in, so thick it seemed to steal the oxygen from her lungs.

She forced herself to speak. "If you think my presence is causing harm, I will step aside from the next gathering," she said quietly. Her own words tasted bitter, but she kept her voice steady. "I don't want to endanger anyone."

Robin turned to her in disbelief. "Ivy, no."

She gave her friend a faint nod. "If it helps the circle stay safe, so be it."

Lucien watched her closely. She thought he might have interjected, but he only inclined his head in an almost imperceptible gesture. She wondered if that was approval or regret. A pang of hurt flared in her chest that he had not defended her more openly.

Selene clasped her hands. "We appreciate your understanding. This arrangement is not permanent. Once we gather more information, we will revisit the matter."

A wave of relief passed among the seers. They began to disperse, some throwing uncertain looks Ivy's way. Dara walked off holding her satchel of dream journals, posture stiff. Cassian gave Ivy the saddest glance before drifting away, his pencil scratching across a new page. Within minutes, the corridor had thinned, leaving only Ivy, Robin, and a few silent watchers by the door. Lucien was already gone.

Robin made a sound of disgust. "They're terrified. They can't make sense of that messed-up symbol you conjured, so they're taking the easy route, blame the outlier."

Ivy exhaled, touching her temples. A dull ache pulsed behind her eyes. "They say it's just until they figure out what went wrong."

"They want a scapegoat," Robin said flatly. "And you're it."

Ivy tried to muster an argument, but the words tangled in her throat. The memory of that weaving session still left her uneasy. She recalled how the threads spasmed when it was her turn. She recalled how light sparked around that embroidered shape, a shape that no one recognized. Maybe the circle was right to keep her at arm's length until they had clarity.

"Let's go, yeah?" Robin's voice softened with concern. "This place feels more haunted than usual."

Ivy nodded, not trusting herself to speak. They walked through the labyrinthine hallway, toward the rear exit of the Chinatown bookstore that masked the Sanctuary's existence. The air outside pricked her cheeks with a crisp bite. Neon signs glowed across the street, and a stray breeze carried the faint smell of sesame oil and incense from a nearby vendor. Ivy realized how tightly she had held her shoulders clamped.

Robin kept a protective hand near her elbow as they walked. "That meeting was unfair. They hammered you with suspicion, all while ignoring that you've never intentionally hurt anyone."

"Maybe I am the variable they should isolate," Ivy said dully. "Not forever. Just until they confirm I'm not making everything worse."

Robin's jaw flexed under the streetlamp's haze. "And what if they decide you are making it worse? Are you supposed to vanish from your own city because they don't like your effect on their precious circle?"

They stopped at the curb. Ivy's heart squeezed. "I don't know," she admitted. "But I need time to think. It's not that I want to be cast out. I just, that ceremony looked so dark when my thread came in. I don't want to do it again if it means harming people."

"Don't let them break you," Robin muttered. "They're the ones messing with powerful forces." Her expression dulled for a moment. "We're going to figure this out, Ivy. I promise."

They made their way to Ivy's apartment, taking a streetcar part of the distance. The city's lights blurred through the windows, each blink reminding Ivy of the weaving's shattered pattern. All at once, she wanted to hide beneath her covers and never step outside. She tightened her coat around her shoulders, ignoring the suspicious looks of a couple who recognized her from local news coverage. Being "The BART Oracle" had once been an odd novelty. Now it felt like a curse.

When they reached her apartment building's door, Ivy paused on the threshold. "Thanks for your help," she said quietly.

Robin's eyes grew gentle. "Let me stay with you tonight. Make sure you don't brood alone."

Ivy managed a faint smile, but she shook her head. "I'll be okay. I promise I'll text if I need you."

Robin held her gaze, searching for any sign of real panic. "All right. But tomorrow, we talk again, yeah?"

"Yeah," Ivy said. "Tomorrow."

She climbed the narrow stairs to her unit, unlocking the door to her small, lamp-lit living space. The quiet of her apartment seemed to welcome her, embracing her with the smell of old books and burnt wax. She turned on a single lamp near the couch. Her gaze landed on the reflection in the dark window, where she half-expected to see a flash of Lucien's pale eyes or that dreadful sigil. She saw only herself.

She sat on the couch, legs drawn up, and laid her wrist across her thigh. The glyph's glow had calmed a little, though it still pulsed in soft intervals, as if it were tapping out a code she could not interpret. She wondered if she should call Ethan. Yet she hesitated. He had enough worries trying to parse the book he found, *The Seer's Reckoning*, the one that hinted at watchers and her name scrawled on old pages. If she called him now, the sting of frustration in her chest might slip through out, and she did not want to be the reason he lost any more sleep.

She clicked off the overhead light and let the dull orange glow of the single lamp hold back the darkness. Her reflection in the window became clearer, a mirror-like silhouette of herself. She studied the faint circles under her eyes and the wariness pressing at the corners of her mouth. The Sanctuary meeting replayed in her mind. Some part of her felt betrayed that Lucien had not stepped in. Another part whispered that maybe he, too, saw the danger she might pose.

Her breaths deepened, echoing in the stillness. She closed her eyes and remembered the moment the woven threads jolted in the circle, snapping around her wrist like little sparks. The symbol that formed had emerged from her own presence. Neither Thalia's gentle energy nor Selene's mirror-laced vision had caused it. That truth weighed heavily on her chest.

Her eyes drifted to the shelf where old diaries, dream-interpretation guides, and a battered notebook of her own scribbles waited in a disorderly stack. She might find some clue if she dug through them, searching for an omen with two eyes and a slash of flame. Yet she could not summon the energy. Instead, she traced the edges of the glyph on her wrist through her sweater sleeve, feeling a warmth that no mere symbol should produce.

For a moment, panic darted through her. Could she truly be the source of the Sanctuary's unraveling? If so, what then? Did it mean she destroy everything she touched? The idea tasted of dread, sour and cold at the back of her throat.

She barely noticed she was speaking until her own voice startled her in the quiet. "What if I..." She stopped, swallowing. She bit her lip, leaving the question unfinished, suspended in the small apartment.

The glyph gave another faint throb, seeming to offer no comfort. Ivy closed her eyes and leaned back against the couch cushions, letting the city lights beyond her window fade. She imagined the circle's distrustful glances, the repeated phrase that it was for her safety. The memory of Robin's anger twisted her insides. The word *unraveling* beat like a drum at the edge of her thoughts.

She took a final, deep breath, trying to banish the night's tension. It refused to leave. She could almost taste it in the air, mingling with the faint pine of her half-burned candle. The moment stretched, heavy and uncertain. She pressed her palm gently to the glyph, as if trying to comfort a frightened animal.

Her voice was scarcely audible in the thick quiet, but it reverberated through every part of her. "What if I am the unraveling?"

SIXTEEN

THE MIRROR CRACKS

Ivy inhaled the stale evening air outside the hidden entrance, a quiet bookstore in Chinatown that concealed the Sanctuary's twisting corridors. The store's cracked sign bent in the faint wind, and though it was well past closing time, she found the back door strangely unlatched. The lock offered no resistance as she twisted the handle. She stepped inside, every nerve wound tight.

A single row of overhead bulbs illuminated the initial hallway, casting a wan glow across battered shelves. Her shoes tapped softly against the stone. She did not belong here tonight. Selene had specifically told her to stay away, and so had others who whispered behind her back, discussing trouble she might cause with her presence. Still, Ivy could not shake the sense that something demanded her return. No matter the warnings, she had to see for herself if the Sanctuary had truly changed, or if she had.

She emerged into a curved corridor beyond the bookstore's interior. The walls felt closer tonight, as if the passage itself had narrowed. Distant echoes of dripping water punctuated the silence. She remembered times when she had walked these halls by Lucien's side, guided by torches. Now the walls bristled with gloom, with none of the mesmerizing wonder she once felt. Instead, shadows clung to every corner, stretching and twisting like silent watchers.

Her glyph, a faint design etched on her wrist, tingled beneath her sleeve. She cupped her hand over it, hoping the warmth of her skin would calm the buzzing pressure that pulsed whenever she was near strong energy. She no longer knew if that energy belonged to her or to the Sanctuary itself.

At an intersection of corridors, a reflection caught her eye. She peered toward a polished panel of glass affixed to the wall. It portrayed a dim version of her face. The lights overhead blinked, causing the reflection to jerk and distort. Ivy's pulse raced. The glass showed her features warping, merging with dark shapes around her until it blinked out of sight entirely. She tried to suppress a tremor in her hand. Perhaps it was an illusion created by her own anxiety, yet she swore she felt someone, or something, watching.

When she forced herself down the corridor, she noticed more mirrors. They lined the walls at intervals, each growing more warped or clouded with faint smears, as though touched by hands that left behind an oily residue. Her steps slowed. She had known these passages to be off-kilter, but not like this. Light bulbs swung from the ceiling on rusted chains, throwing arcs of erratic glow across the mirrored surfaces.

Finally, the corridor opened into the main chamber. Her heart thudded in her chest. This circular room had once felt welcoming, brimming with quiet voices and candlelit gatherings of seers who attempted to glean possibilities from shadows. Tonight, the chamber was deserted. Tall mirrors framed the perimeter, each placed at a slight angle. Their stands wobbled on chipped stone, as if unbalanced by the tension in the place.

A single candelabra on a central table provided a trembling light, the flames too pale to chase away the gloom. The overhead bulbs, set high in the domed ceiling, stuttered in and out, creating the impression of pulses in the darkness. Ivy's footsteps echoed as she snaked around the table. Heat brushed her face, a sudden flush that made her rub her cheeks. The heavy silence pressed on her ears.

Standing there, she noticed a ripple in the tallest mirror against the easternmost wall. Its surface shimmered, then stilled. She took a hesitant step forward. The reflection it showed was not a proper reflection at all. The background behind her was missing, replaced by an emptiness. She swallowed hard. She reached out, her fingertips brushing the cold glass.

In a blink, the mirror's surface cracked in a jagged line, splitting the center of her reflection. The fracture spread in a spiral shape. She drew her hand away, alarm pulsing through her. Pieces of mirrored glass did not fall, and the crack did not remain static. Instead, the shards coalesced, forming an image that contorted her reflection into something else.

A ripple traveled through the entire mirror, as if it had turned to liquid. Her own face blurred, then sharpened into a visage that was unmistakably Lucien's. Pale eyes, an amused curve of his mouth, that cool expression she had come to associate with power. Her chest constricted. She jerked back, wanting to run but feeling rooted in place, compelled to stay by some unspoken demand.

He stared through the mirror, even though it was only a reflection. She swallowed, forcing words out. "Lucien," she said softly, her voice echoing off the stone walls. Her reflection no longer existed. Only his face stared out at her. Her heart hammered.

Footsteps approached behind her. The soft stride was one she recognized. She whirled around to see Lucien in the flesh, stepping through an archway at the perimeter of the chamber. The real man stood with his hands clasped. He wore a collared black shirt, its sleeves unbuttoned at the wrists, exposing the faint pale lines of old, symbolic scars. They glinted in the candlelight. His eyes moved to the cracked mirror and then to her.

"You always find your way back, Ivy," he murmured, his voice smooth and low. "With or without invitation."

She forced air into her lungs, struggling to keep her tone steadier than she felt. "I came to see if the rumors were true. That the Sanctuary's energy is failing. That you, that you're behind something else." She realized she was stumbling over her words, the sense of foreboding pressing in on her mind. "What are you hiding from me?"

He halted near the central table. A reflective polish on the tabletop caught his features, so she briefly saw two Luciens, one real, one ghostlike. His lips curved in a silent half-smile. "Hiding from you? No," he said quietly. "I have never hidden anything you truly needed to know."

She felt anger rising, a rush of hurt that mingled with her recent banishment from certain rites. "Stop playing with words," she said. Her voice bounced off the dome and returned to her. "Everyone is jumpy. They say my presence fractures visions. They say I caused the weave to break at the last ceremony. I need answers."

His gaze moved over her face. Candlelight made his eyes appear almost colorless. "You already know the truth, in part," he replied softly. "You simply need me to say it."

The glyph beneath her sweater sleeve flared with tingling warmth, and she clenched her fingers at her side. She took a breath. "Then say it."

He stepped past the table, each stride bringing him closer until she could make out the faint freckle on his left cheek, the slight lines at his temples that gave him an air of timelessness. "You are not just a Seer," he said, his voice low. "You've always known that, though you doubted. You are a conduit." He paused, letting the word settle into the air between them. "The energy around you stirs and shifts, it does not lie dormant. You do not merely see the future. You shape the path to it."

Her heart pounded so fiercely that the sound filled her inner ears. She stared at him, wanting to deny it, to claim that he was only spinning illusions. Yet a small, frightened part of her believed him. The tide of half-formed premonitions she experienced, the ways other seers' powers surged or broke in her presence, the knotting of threads at the last ceremony, it all pointed to the same conclusion.

She pressed a hand against her chest, as if to steady her racing pulse. "Shape the future," she repeated, struggling to keep her voice from shaking. "That implies I make it happen."

"Not with conscious malice," he answered. "But yes, you give it permission. Your presence unlocks certain pathways for events to unfold. You do not force the outcome, but you allow it to manifest as soon as it appears in your mind."

Her stomach churned. She recalled the fiasco in the circle, how the woven threads had twisted into that double-eyed sigil, how everyone had looked at her as if she were a ticking bomb. The puzzle pieces rearranged in her thoughts, forming a picture far more frightening than any single prophecy. This was not simply about seeing. It was about creation or destruction, depending on how her gift was used.

She backed away as he took another measured step toward her. The flame in the candelabra shuddered, sending shadows dancing around his face. "I don't want that," she said, her voice strained. "I never wanted that. I just wanted to know if what I saw could be prevented. I never meant to open the door for it."

Lucien inclined his head. The shadows seemed to cling to him like an extension of his own presence. "Your desire to prevent harm is precisely why the Sanctuary needed you. Your willingness stands at the edge of possibility. In your hands, the future can twist or right itself."

She bristled. "And what do you want with me? To twist the future for your own ends?" Her thoughts spun as she remembered every subtle push he had made in ceremonies, the quiet manipulations to get her to open herself to the collective visions.

His eyes glinted with an unreadable light. "I have my own aspirations. But I cannot force what you do not allow, Ivy. That is the fulcrum of your gift. We each operate within it."

She forced herself to meet his gaze. She felt an ache in her chest, a tension that curled around her heart. Doubt crept in. Had all of her precautions, all of her attempts to keep people safe, only expedited the dangerous outcomes? The question made her temples throb. "Then I want it to stop," she said, every word trembling with raw desperation. "I can't keep doing this. If my thoughts make these things real, I'll never feel safe again."

He reached her, so close that she could see the faint rise and fall of his chest. She caught the scent of candle smoke and a hint of something metallic that made her recall old ritual knives in the Sanctuary's storerooms. He lifted a hand but did not touch her skin. Instead, he let his palm hover inches from her cheek, as if sampling the energy that radiated from her. Her breath caught in her throat.

He leaned in, and for a frantic moment, she thought he

might kiss her. Instead, his voice caressed her ear. "It already has," he whispered, the warmth of his breath raising fine hairs on the back of her neck. "The rest is echo."

SEVENTEEN

THE TRUTH BENEATH THE TRUTH

I vy felt the conversation even before she heard their voices. The energy in Cassandra's townhouse shifted, carrying a static tension through the corridors like a current. She paused in the kitchen, one hand on the wooden counter where a half-finished cup of tea sat forgotten. A faint, throbbing hum filled her ears. Something was happening in the next room.

She set her tea aside and moved toward the hall, her heart racing. On the opposite end of the corridor, a dusty mirror hung behind a coat rack. Brownish-red stains dotted its gilded frame, and each time Ivy walked by, she tried not to stare at the obscure runes carved around its edges. Now, when she caught a glimpse of it in her peripheral vision, she shivered. It felt as if the runes were staring back, like watchful eyes that had witnessed too many secrets.

Voices drifted from Cassandra's study. Ivy recognized

Ethan's low timbre, tight with anger, and Cassandra's measured response. She hesitated, pressing herself against the wall. Part of her wanted to announce her presence, but a stronger instinct urged her to stay hidden. She needed to understand what had disturbed Ethan so deeply.

"This one is covered in blood," Ethan said, his voice trembling around the edges. "Why do you have a second mirror with runes like that? You've been watching her, haven't you?"

A quiet pause followed, filled with the creak of old floorboards. Ivy imagined Cassandra standing by one of her bookcases, her face calm but guarded. Her aunt often held her arms folded at her waist, reading a situation before replying. Although Ivy couldn't see them, she pictured Ethan's rigid stance, his hands balled at his sides.

"Not watching," Cassandra said in a strained whisper, "guarding. There is a difference."

Ivy inched closer, careful not to let the floorboards betray her. Her pulse hammered at her throat. Ethan never used that accusing tone unless he felt betrayed. Whatever had led him to confront Cassandra so openly must be dire.

"But it is blood," Ethan insisted. "How does guarding her require a mirror stained with blood and runes? It looks like something out of a ritual gone horribly wrong." He paused, and Ivy pictured him raking a hand through his dark, messy hair. "You need to explain, or I swear I'll tell her everything you've been keeping secret."

A measured exhale reached Ivy's ears, followed by a rustling of cloth. Cassandra must have moved across the room. Her next words carried stark gravity, each syllable carefully placed.

"You think I enjoy keeping secrets?" Cassandra asked softly. "I've had no choice. Ivy's power is not simple. It's not mere sight. She is more than a seer. She amplifies the gifts of others, stirs them awake or strains them until they collapse. I've seen it happen before."

Ivy's breath caught. Over the past weeks, she had heard uncertain whispers that she might be something beyond a normal seer. She had felt it during the ceremonies at the Sanctuary, how others' abilities surged or twisted whenever she participated. Yet to hear her aunt declare it so plainly felt like a kick in the chest.

Ethan's response was tight. "Why did you hide this? If she's so dangerous or so important, don't you think she deserves to know?"

Cassandra's tone chilled. "I was not hiding it from her. I was trying to protect her. Her presence can encourage or fracture the power in those around her. That is why Lucien wants her. He cares little about prophecy. He wants her abilities. With her at his side, he would connect to the rest of us as easily as breathing. She is a conduit."

Silence fell, thick and almost suffocating for Ivy. Heat flooded her cheeks, and she had to fight the urge to storm in and demand more clarity. Had Lucien singled her out solely for that ability? The notion made her stomach twist. She pictured his pale eyes in the candlelit gloom of the Sanctuary, how one glance from him always felt too knowing, as though he perceived a hidden spark inside her mind. Maybe he had. Maybe he saw only a tool.

"Does Ivy know any of this?" Ethan finally asked, voice raw. "Does she realize she can break another seer just by being near them?"

Below the quiet conversation, Ivy heard another sound, her own pounding heartbeat. Her aunt's next words felt wreathed in regret.

"She knows an echo of it," Cassandra said. "She has sensed enough to be afraid, but she doesn't know every detail. That mirror is for emergencies, if she loses control and others begin unraveling around her. The runes and blood belong to older wards, old methods of safeguarding entire circles of seers." Her voice trembled. "I prayed we would never need it. I have prayed every day for that."

Ivy couldn't swallow the knot in her throat. The weight of Cassandra's confession settled on her like a heavy cloak. She was a hazard to everyone around her, or she was a potential weapon in Lucien's hands. Either possibility felt devastating.

Ethan let out a harsh breath. "You should have told her. I told you from the start that secrecy would hurt her more than truth."

"And if that truth destroyed her confidence before she could stand on her own?" Cassandra's voice rose. "You saw what happened at the Sanctuary when she tried to weave her thread with the others. They blame her now. They are frightened. She needs courage to face this. And courage, I fear, is brittle when overshadowed by guilt."

Ivy's eyes burned. She recalled the shame surging through her when the threads knotted violently at the séance, the whispered voices calling her the unraveling.

She had never been sure if they were right. Now, Cassandra's words left no room for doubt. Her presence had disrupted everything.

Ethan sounded more subdued. "You call it courage. She calls it feeling alone. At least if she knew, she could make an informed choice. Right now, she's stumbling in the dark, trusting any glimmer that leads her forward, whether it's Lucien or anyone else."

"I understand," Cassandra said softly. "Perhaps we have reached the moment where it is time to tell her everything. But do not forget, each piece of knowledge we uncover puts her in greater danger. Her power is a beacon, and if our enemies gain a foothold, the entire city might pay the price."

The last words dropped like a stone into a still pond. Ivy's shoulders sagged. She had sensed dangers drifting through the corridors of the Sanctuary, in the anxious glances of seers who whispered about converging storms of psychic energy. Yet hearing Cassandra frame it as the city's fate felt crushingly real.

In the next beat, footsteps scraped the floor. "I can't keep this from her," Ethan said. "I won't. She deserves..."

He stopped as if noticing something. Ivy realized with a bolt of panic that he might have caught sight of her shadow. She braced herself, uncertain whether to retreat or reveal herself. But in the flurry of tension, Ethan only made a frustrated noise in his throat and turned for the doorway.

Out of reflex, Ivy stepped back into the kitchen. She heard him stomp into the hall, his footsteps heavy. She expected to see him stride past, but he paused near the threshold, as though forcibly calming himself. A few moments later, he exited the townhouse's front door, giving it a quiet slam. Ivy's pulse crashed in her ears. She dared not move, waiting to see if Cassandra would follow.

The house dipped back into silence broken only by the ticking of a wall clock and the muffled hum of traffic outside. When Ivy finally collected herself enough to stand upright, her legs trembled as though she had run a mile uphill. In that instant, she felt unbearably fragile. She wanted to confront her aunt, but the words tangled in her mind. Cassandra must have sensed Ivy's presence anyway. Cassandra always knew. Yet no footsteps approached, no explanation reached the kitchen.

Ivy gathered her purse and made her way out through the back corridor, leaving Cassandra burdened with her own secrets. Outside, the late afternoon air greeted her with a gust of cool wind that whipped her hair across her face. Clouds pressed low, and the promise of rain hung on the horizon. She pulled her coat tighter and hurried to the street in search of Ethan.

She finally found him standing at the edge of Cassandra's front fence, bent over his phone as if reading something. At the sound of her approach, he startled and shoved the device into his pocket. His gaze turned up, his eyes full of conflicting emotions, relief to see her, guilt at having avoided her, and a leftover sheen of anger from his conversation with Cassandra. For a moment, neither spoke. Then Ethan inhaled sharply.

"There's a café a couple of blocks away," he said. "Let

me walk you there so we can talk." His voice was clipped, still reeling from all he had learned.

Ivy nodded, though she wasn't sure she could handle hearing more. She felt paralyzed by the pieces she had overheard, yet part of her yearned to confirm them. They walked side by side down the sidewalk, letting the billow of the city noise fill the silence. She caught faint whiffs of chili and spices from a nearby restaurant, though her stomach twisted too tightly for hunger.

At the café, they only stayed long enough for Ethan to realize how restless he felt. She watched him shift in his chair, his eyes darting around as a barista pounded espresso. His usual calm remained absent. He looked ready to snap if pressed. Ivy offered no illusions by ordering coffee. Her nerves were fried enough.

"I can't do this here," he muttered, letting out a shaky exhale. "Too many people, too many distractions."

She nodded, setting aside the menu she hadn't even glanced at. Her entire body felt stiff. "We can go to my place," she said softly.

He agreed with a short nod, and they left. The short ride in a rideshare was quiet, with both of them pressed to opposite windows. The glimmer of streetlamps against the tinted glass made Ivy's reflection look pale, her eyes wide with worry. She realized that Ethan likely had even more to say than what she had heard. The knowledge churned in her chest.

By the time they reached her apartment, the sun had slipped behind the Bay, leaving the sky a bruised violet.

She turned on a low lamp, revealing the small living room awash in dim, golden light. Books, half-burned candles, and notepads cluttered most surfaces. Ethan kept his coat on for a moment, as though hesitating to settle in. The tension between them felt strangely fragile.

Eventually, he shrugged off the coat, placed it on a chair, and turned to face her. "I'm sorry," he blurted, pressing his palms over his eyes for an instant. "This is a lot."

Ivy's throat felt raw. She knew she might pretend she hadn't overheard, but a deeper part of her recognized that would do more harm. So she swallowed the lump in her throat and began quietly, "I heard some of what you and Cassandra said."

His shoulders tensed. "You did?"

She nodded. "Enough to know there's a mirror that's supposed to guard me. Or guard others from me. Something like that."

Ethan blew out a breath. He stepped closer, careful not to crowd her. "I did not know until this afternoon that Cassandra had a second mirror," he said. "She wouldn't tell me everything, but the runes, the blood, she finally admitted she's been using it to keep watch. Only she called it 'guarding.' And then she started talking about you being a conduit, about your presence amplifying others' powers."

Ivy sank onto the sofa, letting that weight settle. The thought of her unsuspecting tide of energy fracturing or boosting seers around her made her light-headed. She managed a tight nod, though grief coiled inside her. "She believes that's why Lucien wants me," she murmured. "I guess it explains the times I felt him pushing me to do rituals. He must sense that I magnify his reach."

"Yeah," Ethan said softly, seating himself on the far cushion. "He doesn't care about your predictions. He wants raw power."

Ivy clenched her fists in her lap. She imagined Lucien's voice during the weaving ceremony, how he had guided her hand so gently yet insisted she pour herself into that spool of thread. She hadn't realized how quickly that might have fed him. A chill slid through her, leaving her heart beating faster.

She glanced at Ethan and found him watching her with open concern. The earlier anger around him had softened, replaced by something that looked a lot like heartbreak. "This is too big for me," she whispered, forcing the words out. "I wanted to help people with my visions, not risk turning them into collateral damage."

Ethan's gaze faltered. He reached for her hand, hesitating an inch above her knuckles before gently clasping her fingers. The warmth of his skin eased the tension in her chest.

"You're not turning anyone into damage," he said in a firm tone, but she could tell he was struggling to find the right words. "Cassandra is terrified. She's convinced that telling you everything at once would throw you into panic. Maybe she didn't realize how much she'd hurt you by keeping quiet. Or maybe she just fears Lucien so deeply that she doesn't trust any direct approach."

Ivy swallowed hard and pulled free of his hand. She rose from the sofa, crossing to the low table near the window. Her dream journal lay open there, half a page filled with scribbled notes she had made the previous night. She hadn't looked at it since. She lifted it now and stared at the messy lines describing a city on fire and a set of glowing eyes that lurked behind the flames.

"I can't even interpret my own premonitions anymore," she admitted, her voice hollow. "I used to think I just needed to see them to prevent them. But now everything tangles when I look. And if I'm amplifying or distorting, maybe I'm fueling some catastrophic future instead of stopping it."

A tear hovered in her lashes. She blinked it away, refusing to cry.

Behind her, Ethan's footsteps approached. He stopped at her shoulder, his reflection dimly visible against the window's glass. "Ivy," he said gently. "Why didn't you tell me you felt this undone?"

She shook her head, biting the inside of her cheek. "Because I barely understand it myself." Her pulse echoed in her ears. She turned, letting him see her face etched with worries. "You must think I'm..."

"Don't," he cut in. He reached for her. She let him guide her to the sofa again, her dream journal still clutched in her arms. They sank down together, huddled close in the lamp's faint glow. She braced for more explanations, for him to say that she was dangerous. Instead, Ethan let the silence linger.

His hand settled gently on her knee, a steady anchor in

her muddled thoughts. Gradually, she looked up, meeting his gaze. A solemn resolve shone there, the kind that humbled her. He leaned close.

"Whatever you are," he said quietly, his voice full of layered meaning, "you're still mine to believe in."

EIGHTEEN

CROSSROADS

Ivy pulled the zipper of her jacket higher and tucked her hands into her pockets. The Embarcadero's lamplights cut golden holes through fog that coiled low around the street, but the air still felt bitterly cold. She and Ethan walked side by side, though there was a tension in their silence that pressed against her chest. Her footsteps clicked on the damp pavement. He looked at her several times, hesitating as if trying to find the right words. The watery glimmer of the bay at night might have been beautiful under different circumstances, but now it felt like a great, dark expanse ready to swallow them both.

She stopped near the edge of the pedestrian walkway, looking out at the murky waves lapping against the piers. Her breath drifted in white puffs. The wind carried a faint tang of salt, and an unwanted shiver coursed through her. She couldn't bring herself to face him, her senses attuned to the bristling energy just behind her. They had yet to discuss the warning. From the corner of her eye, she caught how he fiddled anxiously with the strap of his messenger bag.

"Hey," he said softly, stepping closer. His voice was gentle, but that did not ease the tremor in Ivy's stomach. "I need to tell you something important."

She swallowed, feeling her cheeks flush. "Something about me, right? Something Cassandra said?"

He exhaled, and the sound told her everything. Whatever words Cassandra had shared with him, they were loaded with caution and fear. "She told me you're not just a simple seer," he said, his voice tight. "I mean, we already knew about your visions being different, but Ivy, she said your presence magnifies other people's powers."

She tilted her head, fog clinging to her hair in beads of moisture. It felt surreal hearing so direct a sentence describing her life, describing the piece of her she had only recently begun to acknowledge. But there was more. The way he avoided her eyes spoke volumes.

"So I'm not just dangerous to myself?" She forced the question out, each word heavier than the last.

Ethan paused. Steam rose as he exhaled again into the cold air. "You're dangerous to anyone who gets too close," he said quietly. "It can break people, apparently. Amplify them until they lose control. Cassandra said that is the reason Lucien wanted you, why the Sanctuary was both drawn to you and afraid."

The words hammered into Ivy's ribcage. She had sensed the power surging through her whenever she was near other seers, but hearing it put so bluntly stung, and it unleashed a wave of dread. "Dangerous," she repeated, mostly to herself. Then she shook her head miserably. "I don't want to hurt anyone."

He dropped his gaze. His shoulders were tense, as though bracing for a blow. "Cassandra doesn't think you mean to. She says it's just a fact of who you are, and you have a choice in how you handle it. But I, I wasn't sure when to tell you." He moved a step closer, lowering his voice as if the fog itself might overhear. "I'm sorry if this is the worst time to bring it up."

Her throat felt tight, and she bit down on her lower lip to steady herself. Being near Ethan usually kept her calmer, yet right now, the tension between them crackled like static. A surge of anxiety coiled in her heart. The lights of a passing ferry glinted on the incoming tide, but she could not appreciate any beauty as her mind reeled. She pictured the Sanctuary's broken hallways, the haze of incense that used to cling to Lucien's presence, the jarring knowledge that she might have contributed to the unraveling. Now she understood their looks of unease whenever she entered a circle or tried to help with a vision. The very essence of her power could rip them open if they were not guarded.

She drew a shaky breath. "I don't know how to fix that," she whispered. "How do I stop being a threat?"

Ethan reached out, but before his hand could touch her shoulder, she stepped away. The moment his fingertips brushed her jacket, she felt a hint of warmth. It might have comforted her any other time, but right now, guilt and fear layered into one tremendous ache. She needed distance. Her eyes stung with unshed tears, and she hated letting the heaviness in her chest show.

"You're not a threat," he insisted, though his voice shook. "Not to me."

She lifted her arms in exasperation. "Do you even hear yourself, Ethan? Cassandra basically said I amplify people. I cause them to spin out of control, or break them." Her mind moved to the memory of her aunt's warnings, of friends who had once experienced disturbing surges in their abilities around her. It all made sense in a terrible, heartbreaking way. "You might not feel it now, but eventually, maybe it will get to you, too."

He glanced around at the few stray passersby who hurried through the fog, giving them a wide berth. Then he moved closer again, more determined. "I don't believe you automatically destroy everyone," he said. "But you should know the risk, so we can figure out a plan."

She felt tears well up. A plan. A neat solution to the promise of chaos she carried inside. She gave a broken laugh. "I've never had a plan. I've only been stumbling from one crisis to the next." She looked to her left at the quiet bay. The water lapped restlessly, matching the pulse drumming in her ears. "You're telling me I'm basically a loaded weapon around every other seer. Everyone I might care about in that world is in danger just by being near me."

He did not move for a moment, but she felt his intensity in the quiet. Then he nodded. "That's the risk," he said softly. "But, Ivy, you don't have to face it alone."

She heard the plea in his tone, but it only made the

heaviness in her chest tighten further. The knowledge of what she was capable of, or what she might become, loomed like a thundercloud. She hung her head, tears slipping down her cheeks. She just wanted normalcy, or at least relief, and this burden only felt heavier with each day.

Confusion and pain churned in her stomach. She pressed her fist against her mouth to stifle a sob. "I can't," she managed, stepping back. "I can't do this right now."

He tried to catch her arm, but she shook him off, pivoting toward the street behind them. She needed space, air, anything but the endless guilt that threatened to swallow her. The smell of the bay turned sour in her mouth. She heard him call her name, but she walked faster, her footsteps bouncing hollowly against the concrete. Each inhalation felt like a jagged shard of glass in her lungs.

She made her way deeper into the city lights, weaving through pockets of fog that clung to side streets. Along the way, the pang in her chest refused to subside. String lights in the distance looked like ghosts of a festival she could not attend. A moped buzzed past. A homeless man called after her for spare change. Ivy hardly registered either. She had to ask herself the same question again and again. Was she truly a danger? Would people inevitably unravel around her?

Eventually, she ducked inside a 24-hour café where warm light and the scent of coffee provided a brief refuge. She bought a cup of hot tea just to hold something in her cold fingers. She found a seat in the corner, ignoring the startled look of a barista who recognized her from some old newspaper mention. She simply hunched over the steaming cup and let the minute warmth seep into her palms.

She wrestled with the memory of Ethan's face when he said those words. *You're dangerous to anyone who gets too close.* But she also recalled the heartbreaking kindness in his eyes. She could not reconcile how she felt for him, safe, cherished, unexpectedly hopeful, with the reality that her presence might magnify whatever gift he possessed or break him in unseen ways. The weight of the moment made her limbs feel like lead, so she sat there for what felt like an eternity, sipping the plain black tea until it turned tepid.

When she finally ventured outside again, the city was quieter, fewer people moving along the sidewalks. She walked in a haze, not entirely sure which direction she was heading. Accidental glances at reflective windows made her flinch, half expecting to see Lucien's face or some illusions in the glass. She felt haunted by what had been said, and her glyph tattoo on her wrist tingled beneath her sleeve, reminding her that none of this was imaginary.

She ended up at her own apartment building close to midnight, exhaustion soaking through her. She let herself in, shutting the door softly behind her. Darkness pooled in the living room. She did not bother flipping the overhead light. She set down her keys and realized her fingers refused to stop shaking. The earlier conversation echoed in her ears, an unwanted reminder of responsibilities and danger.

Something told her to turn on every lamp, to chase the lurking shadows and unanswered questions from each corner, but she did not follow the impulse. She sank onto the couch with a shaky exhale, burying her face in her hands. If she truly held power that could crack open the minds of others, then how long before more people got hurt? That question gnawed at her.

She considered calling Robin or sending a single text message to let them know she was safe, but her voice felt lost. Instead, she pressed her lips together, silently promising to talk soon, though not tonight. Tonight, she had no words left.

A wave of fatigue pressed down. She kicked off her shoes, still wearing her coat, and stretched out in the darkness. She had half a notion to open her phone and find a message from Ethan, an apology or reassurance, but she could not bring herself to see it, whichever form it took. Eyes shut, she tried to focus on something, anything, besides the ache in her chest.

It happened more quickly than she expected. Her exhaustion slithered into sleep before she could steel herself against possibility. She drifted, sensations detaching from her body, the rhythmic hum of the refrigerator becoming an anchor she could still vaguely hear. But then her consciousness dipped beneath that final tether, and the anchor vanished.

In the dream, she stood in an endless corridor of

shadow, far from the comforting softness of her couch. The darkness felt alive with currents of energy, prickling at her arms. She moved forward, her steps echoing as though the floor were made of polished stone, but she saw no reflection. There was only a faint glow up ahead. She tried to speak, to call out for Ethan or for Robin, but her voice made no sound.

Then she reached two doors. They rose from the corridor walls in front of her, one shimmering as if crafted from clear, fragile glass, the other shaped from pale bone. Both pulsed with separate rhythms of light. The glass door covered in cool silver, while the bone door glowed with a softer ivory luminance. She felt her pulse hammer in her throat.

A pressure built behind her eyes. She stepped closer, reaching out a trembling hand. Before her fingertips could brush the glass handle, the door throbbed with brilliance. She jerked her hand back and turned to the other. Its surface was smooth but carried hairline cracks in the bleached pattern. Neither looked inviting. Neither looked entirely safe.

She became aware of her own breath, ragged with uncertainty. The dream was so vivid she could smell something like old incense in the air, laced with an undertone of decay. She lifted her gaze, searching for any sign, a faint shape, a voice. Nothing. All she had were these two doors, each calling to her with a subtle hum that reverberated through her entire body.

Which would lead her home? She eased her hand forward again, her heart thudding against her ribcage. The silence around her deepened. The instant her fingertip skimmed the glass handle, she heard a distant, echoing cry, her own or someone else's, she could not tell. Light surged across her vision, wiping the corridor away in an avalanche of blinding luminescence.

Her eyes flew open, and she realized she was back on the couch, chest heaving, sweat gathering at the nape of her neck. The living room was dark save for the faint glow of a streetlamp filtering through the blinds. She pressed a shaking hand over her heart. Her entire body felt clammy, as though she had just woken from a fever. But the memory of those doors wouldn't leave her. She felt them still, humming in her consciousness, as if waiting for her to choose.

She forced herself to swallow. Her pulse pounded, and she closed her eyes again, though this time she refused to return to sleep. The vision had not told her which door was right or led anywhere safer than the other. She thought of Ethan's words about being dangerous to anyone who came too close, and a hollow ache formed in her chest. Maybe the doors were simply two ways of breaking her further. She did not know. All she knew was that she had never felt so unsure, so trapped between possibilities that threatened to tear her in half.

Ivy lay there, breathing in shallow gulps, until the night seemed to stretch on without end. In the small apartment, with that vision still pulsing behind her eyelids, she stared at the ceiling. Two doors. One glass, one bone. She could not guess which path led to freedom, or if either one did. And, in that quiet darkness, she truly did not know how to find her way home.

NINETEEN

THE SEER'S ARCHIVE

Ivy stepped onto the cracked sidewalk, fog coiling at her ankles. She paused in front of a worn-out building that bore no sign or plaque except for a single, tarnished symbol embossed near the threshold, a square and compass, so faint it might have gone unnoticed. According to Rowan's cryptic tip, this was once a Masonic lodge. It was said to hide layers of secret rooms far below the surface of the city. Ivy's breath caught as she stared at the worn doors. A heavy padlock secured the rusted handle, daring her to step away. Yet she refused to turn back.

She brushed the alley's shadows with her flashlight, searching for any sign of tampering or a key stashed in the gloom. Her glyph, the tattoo etched on her wrist, pulsed with wary energy. She often felt it flare whenever she was about to cross a threshold that mattered. Tonight, it burned hotter than usual, a stark reminder that she was never entirely alone in her own skin.

Rowan had mentioned a hidden mechanism, some

archaic lever inside the bricks that shifted if pressed with the right intention. Ivy raked her palm across the chilly wall, pressing here, tapping there, feeling for a disguised seam. The air smelled of mildew, old rain, and something metallic. The city's nighttime clamor faded, and her senses turned inward. They told her that the path she needed would present itself, if only she quieted her doubts. She closed her eyes and exhaled slowly.

Sure enough, one of the stones loosened beneath her touch. She pushed with gentle force, and a click reverberated through the doorframe. The padlock slid open on its own, the heavy chain clattering to the ground. Her heart pounded with the thrill of half-known danger. The building's door creaked as she nudged it wide enough to slip inside. The darkness beyond swallowed her flashlight's beam as though starving for light.

She stepped into a short hallway littered with dusty furniture. The place reeked of stale air and years of neglect. She could practically feel echoes of old footsteps and whispered conversations. Ancient Masonic relics, columns, carved wooden chairs, tattered banners, lay scattered among broken shards of plaster. A worn chair slumped against one wall, the upholstery torn and gray.

Her glyph tingled again, urging her onward. She glanced at the phone in her pocket, half-expecting a concerned text from someone, Ethan or Robin. But no phones shone on the screen. She suspected she'd told them little on purpose, needing to do this alone for reasons that felt both personal and necessary.

Cardboard boxes crunched under her boots as she

pushed deeper into the corridor. Toward the end, she noticed a narrow stairwell leading down. A wide sign, once proud, now hung crooked above the descending steps. Its letters had faded to near illegibility, but Ivy could still decipher them. "ARCHIVES." An arrow pointed down into darkness.

She shivered, inhaled, then began her descent. The clang of her footsteps echoed off the stone walls. Each step felt steeper than the last, as if the building were intentionally drawing her down into an ever-deepening crypt. In the silence, she could hear her own heartbeat. She tried to focus on the single reason she had come, the clue Rowan had given, of an archive containing old transcriptions from seers across centuries, perhaps even millennia. She needed answers about her link to Lucien, about the fractured futures that threatened to consume the city and her own mind.

At the bottom of the stairs, she nearly slipped on a slick patch of moss. Water dripped in a maddening rhythm, echoing like a metronome of dread. Shining her flashlight across the path, she spotted a tarnished door, half-ajar, with the same Masonic symbol carved into its center. She swallowed hard and pushed it open.

A single lantern shone inside, perched on a stone pedestal. Dim but steady light revealed rows of shelving along damp walls. Each shelf housed stacks of leatherbound tomes, journals, boxes stuffed with loose papers, and curled parchments. Some volumes were half-disintegrated, their covers eaten away by time or mold. Others looked untouched, preserved with reverent care.

The smell of ancient paper and decaying ink filled the room.

Her heart panged with an anxious excitement. She had found it. The Seer's Archive. Although numerous volumes beckoned her, she felt drawn to a particular set of shelves on the far right, as though an invisible thread tugged her in that direction. She tiptoed across uneven floor stones, the weight of centuries pressing down on her shoulders. Each new breath seemed weighted with dust motes and possibility.

When she reached the shelves, her glyph gave a surge of warmth. Once again, she shut her eyes, letting the pull guide her hands. She brushed her fingertips along the spines of the books. One in particular felt hot against her touch, as if it contained a living spark. Its binding was cracked burgundy leather, the title nearly worn off. She lifted it gingerly, turned it over, and saw a partial inscription. "Transcriptions of Premonitions: 1720–1850." She carried the volume to a nearby table. The worn wood looked steady enough to hold her weight if she leaned on it. Carefully, she set down her flashlight and flipped the book open.

Yellowed pages greeted her, each lined with elaborate handwriting. The first few entries bore names she did not recognize. Mentions of farmland, of old villages, of some unknown coastline that might have belonged to a different era. Then her eyes caught a reference to another seer, further along within the same compilation. Beneath that seer's name, the date read 1762. It recorded a dream of "an endless corridor of mirrors, leading to a man with eyes like polished steel." Multiple sketches in the margins depicted that man's face. Even rendered in hurried ink, it was hauntingly familiar.

Ivy's pulse stuttered. She ran her thumb over the line of text describing those eyes. A prickling sensation marched up her spine. She flipped forward through more scribbled accounts. Time jumped from 1762 to 1780 to 1817, each entry detailing some dire vision. In every instance, that same presence appeared, an unnamed figure with pale, intense eyes. The seers wrote of him using cryptic descriptions, silver gaze, ghostlike posture, an aura of infinite patience. A shiver coiled in her gut as she recognized the portrait forming, Lucien Grey.

She had suspected he was older than he looked. But seeing him surface repeatedly over centuries of seers' recordings tightened an alarm in her chest. She turned more pages. The diaries described disasters, illusions, broken circles, hints of civil strife, signs of entire sanctuaries crumbling. Some entries named him directly. "Lucien Grey leads the Circle astray." It appeared again and again, sometimes scrawled in the margin, sometimes written in trembling block letters across the center of a page. The repeated phrase, "When the world forgets, he returns."

Her breath quickened. These pages felt too real, too close to what she was living now. She turned another leaf, expecting more outlines of bygone tragedies. Instead she froze. The writing she looked upon matched hers exactly. The loops and slants of the letters were identical to the scribbles in her personal journals at home. She saw entire paragraphs describing a city of glass towers, a sweeping bridge, and the taste of salt-laced fog that matched her own city. She blinked quickly, uncertain if her vision was warping. But the pen strokes were undeniably hers, even though the entry's date corresponded to an era long gone.

Her hands shook as she skimmed it. The words depicted a figure with golden-hazel eyes, her exact eye color, standing in a circle of broken mirrors. Then followed a warning. "He stands behind the reflection, always. He cannot be destroyed if the world still beckons him." At the bottom, her own name was signed in the same shape she unconsciously used in daily doodles. She stared, her stomach twisting in knots. How could she have written this centuries ago?

She flipped back to see if there was an explanation. The next page spanned another set of decades, more references to Lucien Grey. She recognized the same ominous phrase. "The one who returns when the world forgets." Ivy pressed her fingers to her temples, fighting a wave of dizziness. She thought of the times Lucien appeared to her in mirrors, his voice slipping through reflections. Now, confronted with these archaic accounts, she understood that this wasn't new. He had been haunting seers for ages, stepping in whenever knowledge of him faded from living memory.

"Dear god," she murmured. Her flashlight's beam trembled across the lines of text. "He's not just old, he's eternal."

The words seemed to echo in the vast silence. Something fluttered behind the final page she had read, like a loose sheet tucked in. She reached in carefully and retrieved a single, thin document, folded so precisely it formed an envelope of old paper. On its surface, the phrase *The Catalyst's Choice* was written in elaborate calligraphy. She opened it. Blank. No words. At the bottom, only her name. Ivy Lewis. The emptiness felt more chilling than any of the dire prophecies she had read. It was as though the page waited for her next move, some choice she had not yet made.

Her breath caught in her throat. She glanced around, half expecting some spirit to materialize beside her or a reflection in the gloom to speak. Nothing stirred. The drip of water from the ceiling was the only sound. She looked back at the folded page, heart pounding.

She could sense a strange current of energy emanating from that blank space, a possibility brimming with either salvation or ruin. All the prior transcriptions spelled out how inevitable Lucien seemed. But the mention of a "catalyst" teased the idea that not every cycle repeated the same way. Perhaps that was her role. Maybe she was not just another seer to be twisted or consumed by him, maybe she was the pivot. The record was incomplete because it hinged on her will.

Taking a slow, steady breath, she folded *The Catalyst's Choice* again and slipped it into the pocket of her coat. The brittle edges crackled in protest, as if aware it was leaving its rightful place.

TWENTY

LOVERS AND LIARS

Ivy jerked awake in the depths of night, a chill rolling through her apartment despite the windows being closed. The lamp on her bedside table stuttered, casting an unsteady glow across the walls. Her heart thudded loudly in her ears. She sensed an intrusion, someone else's presence wandering in her space, even though she recognized no sound of footsteps or locks turning.

She sat upright, pressing a palm over the faint glyph on her wrist. The symbol had cooled in recent days, as though it was trying to protect her from itself. Now it pulsed, sending tiny vibrations along her skin. At that exact moment, the shadows in the corner of her bedroom thickened, becoming tangible, like liquid night pooling against the wall. She bit her lip, her lips already parted by uneven breaths, and tried to push away the wave of dizziness that swept over her.

When Lucien stepped out of that darkness, he emerged with no apology or request for permission. It was as if the air itself parted to accommodate him. She watched him with a mixture of dread and fascination. Dressed in a tailored black coat, he appeared elegant, almost ethereal under the soft lamplight. His silver-blond hair gleamed faintly. In a single glance, he did not look like a wanderer of the city's foggy streets. He looked like he owned the night.

"Ivy," he said quietly, his voice spinning velvet across her already-frayed nerves. "Has your rest been peaceful?"

She swallowed hard, a small tremor shooting through her. "If you're asking whether I've stopped dreaming of you, the answer is no."

Lucien's lips curved into a half-smile, faint and knowing, before he angled his head. "Why are you so unsettled then?"

She inhaled slowly, as if she were trying to steady her racing heart. The shards of her recent talk with Ethan returned to her in a flood, the way he had told her she was dangerous, how even her presence might break those who got too close. Yet Lucien, stepping through the shadows, was never broken by her. He thrived on the chaos she offered.

"You shouldn't be here," she managed, her voice a low rasp.

He lifted an eyebrow. "I could never resist the pull of your thoughts. They echo like a beacon."

Ivy felt an answering pulse in her glyph, as if the rope binding them both grew tighter. She pulled back the sheets, swinging her legs to the floor. The worn hardwood felt cold under her bare feet, but she forced herself to stand.

"You're not welcome," she whispered, but her voice faltered.

Lucien crossed the small space between them with measured pace. His movements radiated silent confidence, and every step made her chest tighten with an odd anticipation she despised. She wanted to speak again, to order him out, but her words vanished.

They studied each other for a long moment in the dim light, the tension thick enough to hitch her breath. Ivy tried to steel herself, but part of her recognized that wave of longing she occasionally hid even from herself. Was it because Lucien was her opposite, someone who reveled in the power she had carefully caged? Or was it the memory of how he had touched her mind through reflections, offering a promise that one day, she would grasp her true potential?

"You've come so far," Lucien said, his voice dropping lower. "And yet, you're still afraid, aren't you?"

She bristled. "I'm not afraid of you."

"No," he agreed softly. "You're afraid of yourself."

An uneasy tremor twisted in her core, and to her horror, she found herself leaning closer, her gaze locked on his.

"You waltz in here expecting what?"

His fingers brushed a stray curl from her forehead, and though his touch was almost maddeningly gentle, her entire body tensed. "I expect you to trust what you really feel," he whispered.

Her lips parted in protest, but the words never came. Lucien's hand slipped lightly to her shoulder, then glided down her arm. The contact sent electricity sparking through her nerves. While every rational instinct howled that she needed to drive him out, physically, if necessary, her body refused to align with that command.

They stood so close that she could breathe in the faint scent of incense and old paper clinging to his coat. His nearness both calmed and ignited her. It was an impossible paradox, being next to the very man who threatened all she fought to protect.

"You should go," she said again, though her tone wavered.

"Ivy," he murmured, fingertips grazing the pulse point at her wrist. "Look at me."

She did. His pale eyes seemed to hold an entire universe, stars too bright, depths too uncharted. He was magnetic, and she found the weight of the night pressing against her as if urging her to close the distance.

Her mind whispered Ethan's name. She saw Ethan's warm, determined face, the safe way he made her feel even when the world rocked beneath her. Guilt spiked. But here, in the silence of her bedroom, Lucien's presence was a different kind of gravity, a pull that made her blood race and her breath catch in her throat.

He bent his head and spoke in a riddling whisper, reciting lines about choice and possibility. She tried to parse the meaning, but the words faded beneath the rising hum of her own heartbeat. Slowly, she tilted her chin up, brushing her gaze against the smooth line of his jaw.

His breath, warm against her skin, was the final impetus. Together, they collided like two storms meeting over a restless sea, their lips finding each other with an urgency she had never allowed herself to feel before. Every nerve in her body came alive. The glyph at her wrist flared, pouring heat across her arm as though acknowledging that, for once, she was not holding back.

Her hands slid up his chest, gathering the lapels of his coat, and she tasted thanksgiving and despair in his kiss. The rational part of her mind tried to lash out, reminding her that this man was the source of so many nightmares. But the rational part was drowned. In that moment, she only felt the wild flood of sensation, as if she were discovering a hidden door inside herself.

They moved together toward the bed, the sheets tangling at their feet. Lamplight streaked across his hair and the pale line of his collarbone when she eased the coat from his shoulders. Cool air skated over her arms, replaced by the warmth of his palms. He trailed his hand across her waist, drawing her against him as though he feared she might vanish.

She whispered something unintelligible, half-lost in the haze, as Lucien's lips traveled along her neck, lingering at the hollow of her throat. He took his time, each reverent press of his mouth unleashing a new wave of heady temptation. She had never known her body could respond like this, each sensation amplified to a near-euphoric level. She shuddered under his hands, hands that teased and caressed as if memorizing the shape of her.

Her breath came in quick gasps. She felt his heartbeat

through the thin layers of clothing still between them. The city's ever-present fog pressed at the windows, and she swore she could taste sea salt on the air. He stilled for a moment, cupping her face gently, and she saw emotions pooling

behind his pale irises, desire, hunger, but also something softer, as though he recognized her fears and wanted to lull them.

Then he kissed her again, deeper this time, and she yielded. Heat curled low in her stomach, spiraling outward. She forgot the hour. She forgot caution. She forgot all the warnings that Cassian, Selene, Cassandra, and everyone else had tried to speak. She forgot that there was another man, across the city, who would stare at his phone wondering if she was safe.

All she knew was this sharp and exquisite moment. The quiet of her bedroom became their world, punctuated by quiet moans and the whisper of blankets. She felt unmoored and powerful all at once. When he traced the curve of her spine, she arched into him, her breath hitching. She had imagined fear might overshadow everything, but instead she discovered a fierce, almost reckless pleasure.

Her glyph burned with that same white-hot intensity she had once fled from, yet tonight, she found herself reveling in the burn. She sensed an echo in Lucien too, a hum that told her he was drawing some sort of energy from her, just as she drew unrestrained bliss from him. They rose and fell in unison, as if the entire city's fog had gathered to cushion them in an otherworldly silence.

Long moments blurred into each other. Whispers mixed with low laughter as their bodies discovered uncharted places, each touch more demanding than the last. She lost track of time, of any identity beyond this collision of unstoppable forces. The bed creaked under their shifting weight, and somewhere behind her, the small lamp on the nightstand glittered dangerously, casting shadows that danced like ghosts against the walls.

When it reached its crescendo, she clung to him, her eyes closed, every sense heightened by the culminating energy between them. She felt more than heard his own release of breath, a stuttered exhale that sounded suspiciously like her name. It surrendered them both to a final swell of rapture and dizzying, soul-twisting satisfaction.

Afterward, she lay dazed, the rapid drumming of her heart slowly coming down to a calmer pace. Lucien's fingertips slid gently along her forearm, playing lightly across the glyph that still glowed warm. Just for a moment, she let herself drift in the afterglow, suspended between guilt and longing.

Her eyelids felt impossibly heavy, and the hum of the outside world, car horns, distant foghorns, the city's night beats, became muffled. She heard Lucien whisper something, his lips touching the curve of her ear, but she couldn't parse the meaning. Soon her mind slipped into a half-sleep, lulled by exhaustion and an odd sense of unspoken comfort.

She did not know when she drifted fully into slumber.

~

MORNING ARRIVED UNANNOUNCED. A silvery-gray light filtered through her blinds, slicing across the bed. Ivy stirred, momentarily disoriented. The sheets stuck to her clammy skin, evidence of hours spent tangling in them. She roused enough to realize she was alone. Lucien had departed the same way he had arrived, like a phantom.

She propped herself up, pressing a hand to her forehead. Her heart felt weighed down, yet her body still hummed with the memory of the night. The strangest part was how profoundly she had needed that moment of release. Guilt flooded her all the same. She had parted her soul to the one man who threatened everything she and Ethan had painstakingly pieced together.

She rose with trembling limbs and stared at her own reflection in the mirror mounted on the closet door. Her hair hung in loose tangles around her shoulders, and the expression on her face was haunted. A flush of shame darkened her cheeks. She rubbed her palms across them, trying to stave off the sense of betrayal that coiled in her chest.

For a moment, she could see Lucien's face in memory, his pale eyes brimming with secrets. She shivered, remembering how reckless she had felt under his touch. She tried to push it aside, focusing her mind on the tangible day ahead.

She dressed in loose lounge pants and a worn sweatshirt, struggling to recapture some normalcy. It wasn't even seven in the morning, but she knew she wouldn't sleep again. Her apartment felt stale, thick with the afterscent of their union. She wanted to fling open the windows but feared the cold air would make her shiver with more than just chill.

A soft rapping sounded at her door. Ivy felt a flash of panic. Then came Robin's voice, muffled by the wood. "Ivy? You home?"

She hesitated, eyeing the bed behind her as if it might reveal everything. But she steeled herself and walked to unlock the door.

Robin let herself in, looking bright-eyed despite the early hour. She wore a big sweater with tattered hems and a pair of slim jeans. Her short cerulean hair stuck out in all directions, and a worried frown marked her face the moment she took in Ivy's appearance.

"Hey, sorry. Your phone was off, and I was, uh, worried," Robin explained, stepping inside. "Did you sleep at all? You look..." She cut herself short when she saw the disarray in the room. The bed was a mess, twisted sheets trailing off one side, pillows on the floor.

Robin's eyes widened in alarm. "Ivy, what happened?"

Ivy tried to speak, but nothing came. She shook her head and gripped the hem of her sweatshirt. That was answer enough. She knew Robin well enough to see the moment they pieced it together.

"Please," Robin whispered, her hands lifting in a questioning motion. "Tell me you didn't."

Ivy couldn't bring herself to speak. She only cast her eyes downward, hugging her arms around her torso. The silence was louder than any confession.

A hint of anger, or perhaps heartbreak, flared in

Robin's gaze. "You realize Ethan loves you, right? You two might not be perfect, but…"

"I know," Ivy choked out, her voice catching. "I don't even know if last night was about love or if it was some twisted part of me that needs that chaos. I…" She broke off, pressing her palm over her face again. A tear slipped down her cheek, and she wiped it away with an impatient gesture.

Robin moved closer, then haltingly placed a comforting hand on Ivy's shoulder. "Hey," she said softly. "All I want to do is help, but I can't if you shut me out."

Ivy exhaled shakily, nodding as if to prove she heard. "I'm sorry," she murmured. "I'm not shutting you out. I'm just drowning, Robin. In everything, my powers, the visions, the fear that I'm losing any sense of right and wrong."

Robin's expression softened. "This city, this circle of seers, Lucien, it's a lot. Still, you have to talk to Ethan. Eventually, I mean. He can't figure things out if…"

"I know," Ivy said. She closed her eyes. For a moment, she expected the glyph on her wrist to flare again in condemnation. Instead, it felt disturbingly calm.

Robin sighed and glanced toward the bed. The rumpled sheets were tinted with morning light, an almost accusatory display of everything that had happened. A quiet spread between them. Finally, Robin stepped back, letting her hand fall to her side.

"I'll give you a minute," she said quietly. "But promise me you won't hide from me too long, okay? I'm on your side, even if I hate what it's doing to you."

Ivy nodded, tears threatening once more. She owed Robin an explanation, but she couldn't muster it now. She could hardly muster an explanation for herself.

Robin gave her one last worried look and slipped back into the hall, gently closing the door. Ivy turned toward the bed, her stomach twisting. The imprint of her body on the mattress seemed illuminated by guilt. She took a hesitant step forward, then paused.

A surge of disgust, or perhaps confusion, rolled through her. She couldn't keep those sheets. They smelled of him, of them, and every time she reentered the room, she would be reminded of how thoroughly she'd let Lucien in. How she'd surrendered her sense of control in that moment. Grabbing the bottom edge of the sheets, she yanked them off the bed in one angry motion. The pillows followed. She hugged the tangle of linen against her chest for all of three seconds before she marched to the small utility closet down the hall.

She shoved the bundle inside, rummaging for a moment until she found a lighter. Stepping onto the narrow balcony that overlooked the alley behind her building, she dropped the sheets in a metal bin that she sometimes used to burn old notes or sensitive documents. The crisp morning air stung her lungs, carrying a faint recollection of salt from the bay.

At first, her fingers struggled to flick the lighter, as though even the cheap plastic mechanism recognized the tension within her. Then, at last, a spark. She touched the small flame to the corner of the crumpled bundle. For a second, the flame threatened to die, but she pressed forward, breathing shallowly. The fabric caught, orange embers creeping over the threadbare cotton. Smoke curled upward, scratching its way into her nose.

She stood back as the fire spread, her arms crossed. The smoky scent made her eyes water, but she refused to step away. She watched the sheets blacken and curl, turning to ash.

As the last of the flame died inside the bin, she swallowed the knot in her throat. She thought of Ethan, his kindness, the way he had once insisted that no matter what power she carried, he would stand beside her. She thought of Lucien, silent and sly, tasting her mouth as if she were the only thing that mattered in the city.

She had chosen an impossible path, no matter where she turned.

Smoke drifted high into the pale morning light and vanished. She stared at the ash, feeling an emptiness that threatened to eclipse her heart. A single vow looped through her mind. She would not lie to herself about what she had done. She would not pretend it was something simple like curiosity or a momentary slip. It cut deeper than that.

TWENTY-ONE

DIVERGENCE

Ivy walked alone along the narrow, crumbling path that led to the abandoned observatory. A late-afternoon gloom clung to the sky, wrapping the cliffs in an eerie silence. Overhead, gulls circled, their shrill cries swallowed by the wind. She pulled her coat closer, though the fabric was too thin to shield her from the chill that seeped into her bones.

She arrived at a hollowed archway where the gate once stood. Years ago, she had strolled here with raw curiosity, thrilled by the quiet inside the dome. Now, she slipped through the half-collapsed entrance, her heartbeat echoing in the deserted corridors. The old observatory smelled of salt and moss. Sections of the ceiling had caved in, letting in streaks of pale light. She chose a spot by one of the side walls, dwarfed by the gaping emptiness where a massive telescope once rose. She remembered how, in better days, children lined up to peer through that telescope at stars. It felt like a lifetime ago.

Here, she noticed no visions, no voices pressing against her consciousness. Her power lay quiet, as though it could not cross the threshold into this place. This had always been her retreat. As a teenager, she had come with a sleeping bag and a notebook, hoping the silence would settle her restless mind. Tonight, her mind spun with memories, the crack of a shattered mirror, her reflection turning into Lucien's calm, predatory gaze, and Cassandra's tense warnings about her abilities. She pressed her forehead against the wall, frustration raking through her.

She did not want to be a conduit, did not want to be so inescapably tied to the future. She remembered her aunt's confession that Ivy's presence amplified or fractured others' gifts. She had felt it in recent days. Her mere presence churned the Sanctuary's calm into disarray. She squeezed her eyes shut, wishing she could simply unlearn every dreadful truth. But truth clung to her like a brand.

By the time night fell, a haze of exhaustion settled over her. Gray clouds smothered the last band of sunset. She huddled on a half-broken bench near the outer rim of the dome, her arms wrapped around her knees. Her phone, stashed in her bag, stayed off. She could guess that Cassandra or Ethan had tried to reach her. Maybe even Robin. Guilt gnawed at her, but she could not summon the energy to go back. If returning meant facing more worried expressions or more half-answers about her destiny, she would rather remain in the solitude of this place.

At some point, fatigue overcame her. She dozed off, shoulders hunched, lulled by the wind that whistled through the gaps in the observatory's structure. She woke several times in the night, startled by the drip of water or the groan of rusted beams. Each time, she checked for visions in the corners of her mind. Nothing appeared, filling her with both relief and loneliness. Perhaps she had wanted a sign. Perhaps some part of her thirsted for clarity, despite her fear. Yet the observatory offered only silence.

When she rose at dawn, her joints stiffened from cold. She paced the perimeter, her footsteps crunching over fallen plaster. She looked out through a broken arched window at the ocean. Fog blurred the horizon, merging sea and sky into a single gray mass. She caught her reflection in a chunk of broken glass embedded in the rubble. Her hair hung in disarray around her face, and her eyes were rimmed with weariness. It scared her to see how vacant she appeared, as though a shadow had settled behind her gaze.

She crouched and traced her fingertips over the fractured glass. She did not realize she was crying until tears fell across her knuckles. They came quietly, twisting through her chest with dull ache. She pressed her palms hard against the rough floor, trying to find an anchor to hold her. She had never felt so uncertain that she deserved to exist among people who looked to her for hope. She did not even know if she could touch them without warping their lives.

She started mumbling to herself, her voice breaking. "I should never have meddled," she said. "I can't keep doing this." The words echoed in the cavernous emptiness.

Hours passed in a blur. The cold intensified. Her

stomach rumbled, reminding her she had eaten nothing since the previous morning. She had no plan for what came next. She only knew she needed to stay where the visions could not follow her. Each time she heard a distant echo outside, a footstep or the scrape of debris in the corridor, her chest clenched with apprehension. She expected to see Ethan's silhouette or Cassandra's austere figure. But no one entered. She was alone.

Then, by late afternoon, she heard a lighter, hurried footfall. Startled, she pressed herself against a pillar, reluctant to be found. The footsteps paused, then continued with determined purpose. Ivy's pulse quickened. After another hesitant moment, Robin emerged through a side arch, her eyes scanning the debris-strewn floor.

Robin wore an oversized sweatshirt beneath a worn jacket, with a scarf that flapped in the wind. Her eyebrows shot up in relief the instant she spotted Ivy. "Oh, thank God," Robin breathed, rushing forward. "You had me freaking out. I was sure you were in danger. I've been searching everywhere."

Ivy opened her mouth to speak, but the words stuck. She managed a small nod, her arms locked around her torso. Robin was breathing hard, her cheeks flushed, their hair tufted in multiple directions. Concern shone plainly in their eyes.

"I thought about texting," Ivy said softly. "But I couldn't, I couldn't handle everything right now."

Robin nodded. "I get it. But let's get you out of this cold." She reached for Ivy's hand, but Ivy pulled backward, as though fearful of harming them with a single touch. Robin's expression bore a quiet heartbreak at the rejection.

"I'm not trying to push you," Robin said, gentler now. "I know you've had a rough time. I just want to help."

Ivy's breath shuddered. "I can't un-know the things I've learned. I keep hearing everyone else's warnings in my head. Cassandra, Ethan, Lucien, it's all muddling. I want to undo it all. I want to not be this person who spills chaos just by existing." Her voice cracked. She blinked fiercely, tears returning.

Robin studied her, the silence stretching. The wind rattled overhead, knocking a loose shingle off the dome. It clanged on concrete. After a moment, Robin braced a hand lightly on Ivy's shoulder. When Ivy did not flinch, Robin pulled her closer, slipping both arms around her in a fierce hug. Ivy cried into her friend's shoulder, half-ashamed at how badly she needed the contact.

"You can't un-know things," Ivy whispered, echoing the thought consuming her. She gave a broken laugh that caught on a sob. "And I'm starting to think I was never meant to know anything."

Robin's embrace tightened. Her voice came out in a determined whisper. "If it's too heavy," Robin said, "then let me carry some of it for a while." She stroked Ivy's hair, the gesture both protective and comforting. "You've been wrestling with this alone for too long."

A soft sniffle escaped Ivy. "I don't want to hurt anyone. If what Cassandra said is true, if I can break other seers by amplifying them to the point of danger..." She choked on the memory of ceremonies gone awry and the echoes of fear in people's eyes.

Robin shook her head firmly. "No one out there is safer without you. They need you. You have gifts that are real, no matter how messy they are. And guess what, I'd bet all my vinyl records that your messy gifts are not the problem. Every single seer I've met has baggage. Yours might be bigger, but it's still part of who you are."

Ivy exhaled a shaky breath, her tears still wet on her cheeks. She realized how numb her hands had become, and so she let Robin pull her deeper into the half-intact structure, where wind did not slice quite as hard. Her friend found a relatively sheltered corner with an angled piece of broken wall that offered partial protection. Carefully, Robin coaxed her to sit.

From a small backpack, Robin produced half a wrapped sandwich and a thermos of lukewarm tea. "You should eat something," she said, pressing the sandwich into Ivy's hands.

Ivy stared at it, the tang of cheddar mingling with the stale, cold air. She took a small bite out of obligation and discovered that she was starving. She quickly devoured the rest. Robin watched, half-smiling in relief. While she finished, a deep silence settled. Outside, the sky darkened as dusk approached. In the gloom, Robin fished an emergency blanket from their bag. They draped it over Ivy's shoulders. The reflective silver rustled, but the warmth was immediate, soothing some of the tension in her muscles.

"Thank you," Ivy murmured. She wiped her mouth,

her eyes darting toward the ruined telescope mount a few feet away. "I came here because they can't reach me when I'm in this place. The visions, the illusions, they all go quiet." She paused, swallowing. "It's selfish, but I needed quiet."

Robin nodded. "Needing peace isn't selfish."

"That's the thing," Ivy replied, her voice tight. "Every time I think I understand what's happening, I learn something worse. The moment I try to help, I unravel people's powers or feed their gifts until they break. I can't figure out if I'm more dangerous than Lucien or if I'm just a puzzle piece in his game." She closed her eyes. "You didn't hear what he told me. He said I shape the path to the future. That I give it permission." The last word trembled in the space behind her teeth.

Robin laid a hand on her hand, pressing gently. "I wish I could promise you it'll be easy. I can't. But I can promise you're not alone. If you don't want to do any more group visions or ceremonies, then don't. We can figure out another way. You have people who care about you. You have Ethan, Cassandra, me... we're not going anywhere."

Ivy opened her eyes, fresh tears threatening. She nodded slowly. "I don't know what I am anymore," she said. "But I know who I want beside me when I find out."

Robin squeezed her hand in response, not letting go. They sat like that, shoulders touching, until the sky had darkened completely. The night air carried extra bite, so they retreated even further into the remains of the observatory to shield themselves from the gusts. Robin regaled her with an exaggerated tale about searching half of *San Francisco* for any clue to her whereabouts. They sprinkled in remarks about the clueless clerk at a gas station or a random dog that nearly followed them onto a bus, coaxing the hint of a smile from Ivy. She realized how comforting it felt to let someone else ramble, to let the weight of conversation rest on another pair of shoulders.

They slept fitfully that night, side by side against the least broken section of the wall. Robin's emergency blanket crinkled each time they shifted. Ivy drifted in and out of uneasy slumber, more at peace than she had been alone, though the sorrow in her chest lingered. She thanked the old walls for blocking any intrusive visions, for silencing the hum she often felt when too many forces pulled at her mind.

When morning's first light crept in through a fractured skylight, Ivy stirred. The white glow illuminated the collapsed interior of the dome. Her breath showed in small puffs. She found her journal in her bag, rummaging past the phone she still refused to turn on. Then, leaning against a broken ledge, she started writing. The nib of her pen scratched across the page. Her words came unsteady, shaped by exhaustion and a faint, sorrowful clarity.

I don't know what I am anymore. But I know who I want beside me when I find out.

She read the sentence, her heart pounding gently. That was enough. She had not solved her predicament. She had not mended the city or answered Cassandra's warnings.

But she felt a sense of purpose. She pressed the journal against her chest.

Robin stirred from a half-sleep, blinking in the dull glow. "Writing a new prophecy?" she teased softly, their voice rasping from the cold.

Ivy shook her head. "No," she said. "Just writing what I need to remember."

Robin raked a hand through their hair, sat up, and offered a faint grin. "We should get you home," she said. "A real bed, warmth, probably some demands from certain people who love you. But I'll help you face them."

Ivy's throat tightened with gratitude. Despite the numbness in her fingers, she clutched the journal and nodded. "I'm ready."

Wordlessly, Robin helped her stand. They picked their way through the fallen stones and out into the morning wind. The ocean glinted in the distance. Ivy's coat flapped behind her as they climbed the chiseled footpath and emerged onto the gravel lot above. Clouds hung low over the cliffs, but faint sunlight peeked through. Without a word, they walked to Robin's small, worn car.

Robin opened the passenger door. Ivy sank into the seat, wrapping the emergency blanket more tightly around herself. The engine coughed to life, and she watched the ruined observatory recede in the rearview mirror. For a moment, she felt a pang of loss at leaving the one place that quieted her gifts. Still, she made her choice. She would return. She would face whatever came next, as long as she did not have to face it alone.

Robin drove away from the cliffs, guiding the car down

winding roads that led back to the city. The sun pushed through a thin layer of fog, illuminating the rolling hills in pale gold. A new day beckoned, uncertain but undeniably present. Ivy closed her eyes, pressing her palm to the journal in her lap. She breathed in, letting the tension ease from her shoulders.

They were going home.

CHAPTER

TWENTY-TWO

THE SLEEP THAT SEES

Ivy curled onto her side, hugging the last cushion on her couch as the moonlight crept through half-drawn curtains. She had done everything to avoid sleeping, brewed another pot of tea, paced the living room, reorganized the small array of crystals on the windowsill. But exhaustion pressed down on her. Every muscle ached from tension that refused to dissipate. Even the glyph tattooed on her wrist throbbed with a slow burn, as though it held a fever she could not sweat out.

The city's muffled clamor provided little comfort. Horns droned in the far distance, and the occasional gush of wind rattled the windowpane. Finally, around midnight, she surrendered. She dimmed the lamp, letting the apartment sink into a quiet broken only by her uncertain breathing. Then she lay back on her pillow, pulled a knitted throw across her shoulders, and closed her eyes.

Sleep came in fragments, bringing no relief. The vision started abruptly, dragging her consciousness into a world illuminated by flames. She stood in the center of a dark rooftop, though she did not recognize which building it might be. Fire coiled around the edges of her sight, licking at the horizon as if the entire city were on the brink of burning. An acrid tang filled the air, hot metal, singed fabric, the pungent reek of something more final than mere destruction.

She tried to breathe, but her lungs felt thick and slow, and her heart hammered as if urging her to turn away. Except there was no escape. A towering pyre rose in front of her, built from shattered beams and remnants of wood half soaked in oil. Flames licked upward in lazy columns of red and gold. The heat pulsed against her face, enough to make her skin prickle with sweat. Somewhere behind that fire, she saw a silhouette. Tall, proud posture, hands folded with eerie stillness. A voice, Cassandra's, traveled on the crackle of kindling.

"Ivy?" Cassandra's call echoed, wavering. Her aunt's voice held both sorrow and urgency, as though Cassandra herself were beyond the barrier of flame. Ivy wanted to shout back, but the words stuck in her throat.

Then the air cracked. Her gaze jumped from the pyre to the edge of the rooftop. Ethan stood there, on the other side of a shimmering veil that seemed to slice the very space between them. He reached one hand forward, but the membrane refused to let him pass. She saw him mouth something, her name, maybe. She rushed toward him, each step forcing her through waves of blistering heat. The veil shuddered like a half-lit reflection. Just when she drew near enough to see Ethan's eyes, an unseen force yanked her backward.

She cried out as the funeral pyre brightened, blazing as though it responded to her pain. Wood snapped and collapsed into a heap of embers. In that rush of sparks, she heard Lucien's low, resonant voice weave through the flames.

"This is one version," he said. His presence materialized at her shoulder, close enough that she felt his breath. "But you know there are others."

She spun to face him, words shredding in her throat. The flames surged, swallowing her vision in hot, rolling fury. In the dazzling red, all she could see was Lucien's silhouette leaning toward her with a calm that sent panic through her chest. She was certain he would pull her into that inferno. Then darkness slammed down, quenching the fire as if some cosmic hand had flipped a switch.

Silence followed. Not the silence of peace, but a stifled quiet that thudded in her ears. She tried to inhale, but the blackness weighed her down.

When she woke, she lurched upright, gasping so frantically her ribs seemed to lock. The transition from the inferno's heat to her living room's chilly air hit her like a shock. Her body felt alien, her limbs thick and cold, sweat dampening the nape of her neck. She brushed her hand over her chest, trying to slow the rabbit-fast hammer of her heart, and realized her fingertips trembled enough to make her nails click softly.

For a moment, confusion reigned. She couldn't remember falling asleep or shifting to lie sprawled across the floor. The blanket was half-pushed away, twisted around her feet. The overhead light was off, and only the dim city glow leaked from behind the drapes. Her mouth tasted of copper, as though she'd bitten her tongue. Her pulse roared in her ears.

She sucked in air, trying to focus, to ground herself. Yet something in the corner of the room moved. She jolted, her eyes wide. A shadowy shape wavered, just beyond her line of vision near the coat rack. She blinked, her chest tight. The shape did not vanish. Instead, it swayed, as if aware of her attention. Her glyph burned with sudden intensity, a searing line of heat across her wrist.

She forced herself to look away from the corner and down at the tattoo. It nearly glowed in the faint darkness, each delicate stroke outlined in an incandescent shimmer. The sensation was not just warmth. It felt alive, pulsing with a heartbeat that matched her own.

Then she felt it, a presence inside her mind, like a half-formed memory that did not belong. She pressed a hand to her forehead, trying to steady the wave of dizziness that threatened to topple her. She was not alone in her own body, or so it seemed. The thought made her skin crawl with dread.

Her phone lay on the coffee table. She lunged for it, ignoring how the quick movement sent dizziness spiking behind her eyes. If something else lingered here, she needed help. She needed Ethan.

She fumbled the phone, nearly dropping it as she called him. It rang three times, each chime echoing in her ears before his voice emerged, laced with groggy concern.

"Ivy?" he asked. "What happened?"

"Can, can you come over?" she whispered, pressing the phone hard against her ear. "Please."

He must have heard the fear in her voice because he said nothing more, only a tight exhalation before promising to be there. The line disconnected. A wave of relief and guilt churned inside her. She hated needing him so desperately, but she couldn't face the crawling darkness alone.

In the silent minutes that followed, the shadow remained by the corner, unmoving. She refused to look directly at it, focusing instead on the rhythmic beep of streetlights outside to anchor her. The door eventually rattled with Ethan's brisk knock, and she scrambled to open it so quickly, she nearly tripped over the blanket tangling her ankles.

He stepped inside, his chest heaving like he had run the entire way. His hair was disheveled, a hastily thrown jacket hanging from one arm. The instant his eyes landed on her, his worried frown deepened.

"What's going on?" he asked, low-voiced. "Ivy, you look pale."

She grasped his shirt, guiding him inside and kicking the door shut. The moment he set the deadbolt, she exhaled in a trembling rush. She wanted to explain everything, the funeral pyre, Cassandra's voice, Lucien's words thick with menace. But her thoughts still reeled, bearing the imprint of that vision. Instead of speaking, she led him to the couch. The overhead light buzzed faintly when she turned it on, pushing the shadows to the perimeter like cornered animals.

"I saw something. It wasn't just a dream," she managed at last, her voice faint. "I felt the heat of that fire. Cassandra was calling for me, and I couldn't reach her. Ethan..." She paused, forcing calm into her next words. "I tried to find you, but you were on the other side of a veil or a barrier. And then Lucien." Her voice shook at the memory. "He said it was one version. One possible future. It felt so real, as if it was happening right now."

He pressed his hand over hers, noting how her fingers quivered. "This shadow in the corner, is it part of this vision?"

She nodded, pressing her lips together. "It's still there. I see it, or feel it. The glyph on my wrist is burning, and something keeps tugging at the edge of my mind. Like I brought back a piece of that nightmare."

Ethan's jaw tightened. He rose in one smooth motion, stepping across the small living room. He flipped the overhead switch a second time, flooding the space with brighter light. The sudden glare made Ivy flinch, but she strained to watch him scan the corner. He reached a hand forward, as if to wave through empty space.

"There's nothing here," he said quietly, turning back to her. "No one."

But Ivy knew that was not strictly true. Whatever lingered was intangible. It resided in the leftover vibrations of the vision. She swallowed, tears burning her eyes.

Ethan returned, kneeling in front of the couch. He gently captured her wrists, his thumbs brushing the spot where the glyph glowed. She felt his warmth seep into her, a welcome tether. "Tell me what to do," he murmured.

"You're doing it," she choked out, tears slipping down her cheeks. Embarrassment curled her insides, but relief overwhelmed it. She needed his presence to erase the heaviness that had clung to her since she woke.

He guided her closer, and she sank to the floor beside him, her knees bumping against his. He cradled her palms in his, leaning in so his forehead nearly touched hers. "Breathe," he said softly. "I've got you."

She let out a breath shuddering with pent-up fear. His lips brushed her temple, a gentle reassurance that soothed the static in her mind. Their kiss began with careful comfort, a quiet meeting as if warding away the last tendrils of darkness. But the moment his mouth slanted more firmly against hers, she felt a rush of need flare inside her. Something about being this close to him grounded her more effectively than any incantation or protective talisman ever could. She slid her hands around his shoulders, drinking in the reassurance of his body's warmth amid the lingering chill in her veins.

"Stay," she whispered, her voice hoarse. She did not clarify if she meant for the night or for longer. He stood, lifting her with him, and they moved to the bedroom with unspoken urgency. The overhead lights she had left burning cast a glow along the hallway, but the deeper shadows lingered at the edges of her vision. She held Ethan's hand tightly, refusing to let the darkness claim any more of her.

They stumbled into the bedroom, their breath

mingling in desperation. Clothes fell aside in quick, awkward motions. Maybe they were both just trying to outrun her terror. Yet, when Ethan pulled her against his chest, slowing his movements, she realized it was more than that, a tenderness rooted in the affection neither had ever dared to voice plainly, the trust that had grown despite all the secrets festering around them.

Their previous night together had been ignited by fear and vulnerability as well, but tonight felt different. Tonight, she needed to feel safe. He pressed his lips to her throat, his arms strong around her waist, and she sighed into his hold. She threaded her fingers through his hair, guiding his mouth toward hers again, letting the sensation of his heartbeat steady what still shook in her.

She lost herself in the urgent rhythm of their bodies. Each touch became a promise that the horrors of her visions, or the strange shadow waiting in the living room, would not take her mind. Her pulse thundered in time with his, and she anchored herself in every gentle press of his hand against her skin. At one point, the glyph on her wrist sparked so hotly that she gasped, but Ethan's lips found hers in a soothing caress, and she melted into the closeness of him.

The ache of fear eased. She surrendered to a slow, smoldering warmth curling through her belly, one that pooled and then burst into a cascade of sensation. When she finally stilled, her muscles trembling from release, she pressed her face to the crook of his neck, and the quiet afterglow enveloped them like a cocoon. Their breathing mingled, and for the first time in hours, she felt the frantic edge in her chest recede. Only a faint spark remained in her glyph, as if lulled by intimacy.

He brushed a hand through her hair, gently tugging away any tangles. "Are you okay?" he asked, his voice husky. "I mean, better?"

She nodded, pressing a soft kiss to his shoulder. "I think so." It was not a solution, she knew, but it was a salve, for now. The creeping menace that had followed her from the dream still lurked somewhere in the back of her mind, but she felt safer with Ethan here.

TWENTY-THREE

THE BROKEN CIRCLE

Ivy paused at the dimly lit entrance to the Sanctuary, her heart thudding as she sensed something was off. Typically, even in tense moments, the corridors hummed with quiet conversation or the soft rustle of pages turning as seers pored over archives. Now the great double doors stood ajar, their heavy iron hinges squeaking with each uncertain breeze. A quiet lay over the place, almost funereal.

She adjusted the strap of her worn tote bag against her shoulder, steeled herself, and stepped inside. Her glyph felt curiously cold on her wrist, and she stroked a thumb across it as if trying to reassure it, and herself, that they had come here with purpose. The usual line of candles that guided visitors down the main passage were snuffed out, only a few stubs remaining. She turned on the small flashlight in her bag and scanned the hall.

Empty benches lined the walls, and scraps of parchment lay scattered across the floor. She recognized a few pages from the seer logs, scribbled notes about shared visions or illusions. The place felt ransacked, as though a storm had plowed through. Even the heavy tapestry that once hung beside the library entrance was gone, exposing rough patches of stone. The sweet incense that typically perfumed the hall was replaced by the acrid scent of fear.

Ivy swallowed. She had heard rumors milling all morning that Thalia and Selene vanished in the dark of night. No formal announcement. No farewell. Yet the silence heavy in the air suggested everyone else was well aware. As she advanced, her next step crunched onto a piece of shattered mirror. She nearly slipped. After regaining her balance, she stooped to examine the shards. Thin hairline cracks along the edges indicated it had not merely fallen but exploded. A trickle of unease coiled through her stomach.

Rounding the corner, she found Cassian alone, slumped on the floor near the deserted gathering chamber. His hoodie dwarfed his wiry frame, and he was hugging his knees to his chest. On the stone beside him lay pages from his sketchbook, pages hastily torn, the scrawled images making no sense at first glance. She could make out jagged lines, half-formed shapes like windows or doorways, and frantic scribbles that overlapped again and again.

"Cassian," she called gently, lowering herself into a crouch next to him. "Hey. It's, it's Ivy. Where is everyone?"

He lifted his head. His eyes were rimmed red, as if he had been crying. The sight crushed her heart. He normally hardly spoke, but his sketches often said more than words. Tonight, he only stared at her, his mouth trembling.

"Gone," he mumbled. "Thalia and Selene, they left. Maybe they were pulled away. I don't know." His fingers tightened around the edge of one torn page. "They blamed you. At least some did. I heard them."

Ivy's chest tightened. Her thoughts flooded with images of whispered conversations, suspicious glances, the heightened tension that had followed her every step since she had left the Sanctuary late the night before. She couldn't ignore the reason. People believed she had aligned herself with Lucien. At that recollection, she felt heat flare low in her belly, guilt, longing, confusion. It stained her cheeks to think about how she had let him in. There was no easy way to erase that.

"Look, I don't know all the details," she said, her voice unsteady. "But the Sanctuary is bigger than any single rumor. Please, stay calm, Cassian. I promise I'm trying to fix what's happening."

He pressed a hand over his face, tears springing again. "I see it splintering," he whispered. "Lines ripping us apart. I sketched it last week. Thalia, Selene, you, everyone scattering like dust. I couldn't stop it."

She inched closer, carefully placing a hand on his shoulder. "We won't give up. This place, this circle, was meant to bring people together, not force them aside. You are not alone."

Cassian looked at her for a long few seconds, his eyes brimming with anguish, then abruptly clutched his sketches and stumbled to his feet. Without another word, he lurched down the hall, leaving Ivy alone in the half-light. A few stray pieces of paper trailed after him, catching on the cold stone floor.

Ivy exhaled and stood, pressing her hands against her temples to quell a rising headache. She took a shaky breath. All day, rumors had followed her like crows. She'd heard them at the café, in the whisper of phone calls. "Ivy's sided with Lucien... She's given him the key to every fragile mind among us... She's chosen him." The words sank into people's thoughts, turning them suspicious and fearful. Though her encounter with Lucien had been a night of messy impulse, it had sown deep doubt in every direction.

Footsteps echoed suddenly behind her. She pivoted to see Ethan approaching from the far side of the corridor. He wore the same navy jacket he always did, but tonight it was rumpled, as though he had spent hours pacing or wrestling with indecision. His hair stuck up in uneven spikes, and his jaw was set with tension. The moment she saw him, her throat tightened.

"Ethan." She tried to keep her voice calm, yet a trembling edge betrayed her. "I'm glad you're here. I don't think..."

"Don't say you don't think," he cut in, not loudly, but with a rawness that sliced through the quiet. "I've been hearing it all day. Lucien's name on everyone's lips, rumors that you..." He stopped, shaking his head. "They say you gave yourself to him. Is that true?"

A flush of shame heated her neck. "That's complicated." She couldn't bring herself to outright deny it.

Couldn't shape a neat explanation of what it had meant or how she had let everything spiral. "I…"

He took a step closer, and for a heartbeat she thought he might reach for her hand. Instead, his fists stayed clenched at his sides. "You asked me to trust you," he said, his voice trembling with hurt. "You said we were a team. Then Lucien shows up, and you vanish into the night with him. Now people think you've turned your back on everything you claimed to believe in."

"It's not like that," she whispered. "You have to understand, there is a pull between Lucien and me that has nothing to do with logic. My powers react to him. But it doesn't mean I choose him. It doesn't mean I've thrown my loyalty away. I don't even, I don't know what it means. Except I'm not out to destroy us."

A muscle jumped in his jaw. "He's toxic, Ivy. You know that, right? He's undermining the entire circle. People are disappearing, or else they're being taken in by his illusions. Thalia and Selene gone, Cassian half-catatonic, how much more proof do you need?"

She inhaled, forcing herself to look him in the eye. "I'm trying to keep this place from collapsing. You have no idea how torn I am. It's like my presence is ripping everything in half. I never asked for that."

He stared at her, frustration and heartbreak mingling in his gaze. "Then fight it. Or push him away. If you keep dancing between sides, you're only fueling the chaos."

His words stung, and she drew back as if struck. "You think I want to be trapped in the middle of this? I'm not 'dancing' between sides. Lucien's not my master, and I'm not your puppet. I'm a person who's stuck with a power that's threatening everyone I love. Don't you get it?"

He ran a hand through his hair. "Then whose side are you on? Do you even know anymore?"

Her heart pounded so hard she thought it might crack her ribs. Anger, sorrow, and exhaustion collided in her mind, making lightning sparks behind her eyes. "Sides? Look around, Ethan. There are no sides. Just fallout."

That single statement hung in the stale air. She saw something shutter in his expression, as if her exhaustion had snapped the last thread of his hope. He hovered there, his gaze full of an ache that matched her own. Then he stepped away.

"Fine," he said, his voice hollow. "If you can't decide, I can't force you. But I won't stand here while everything you and I tried to build goes down in flames." Swallowing, he started backing down the corridor, his footsteps echoing. He paused once more, looking at her as if he wanted to say something else. Instead, he turned and walked away.

Ivy's throat felt tight, tears burning behind her eyes. She stood perfectly still, letting his footsteps fade. She feared that if she chased after him, she would break something else beyond repair. But letting him go felt like giving up the only anchor she had left.

Silence swallowed the hallway again. Reality settled in. The Sanctuary splitting at the seams, trust shattered, and now Ethan's heartbreak throbbing in the gulf between them. In the distance, she heard Cassian's ragged sobs echo faintly. She knew she should comfort him. Yet she felt paralyzed by her own guilt and frustration.

Deep in her chest, the glyph gave a reluctant flutter. She could almost swear it was urging her to move. To do something rather than stand in the wreckage, anything to keep from crumbling under her own uncertainty. She pressed her lips together, inhaling through her nose. If no one else would fix what was happening, maybe she had to try, alone if necessary.

She whirled around and retraced her steps down a side corridor rarely used. Her flashlight bobbed in the darkness. She passed two more sets of closed doors, each typically leading to quiet reflection rooms or study alcoves. Both stood open now, as though the inhabitants had fled, leaving chairs overturned and the occasional waver of spent candles on the floor.

She kept going, adrenaline picking up in her veins. Dust motes danced through the beam of light, highlighting a passageway to the right she had never noticed. The stones around the archway looked older than the rest, pitted with time. An unlit torch bracketed the right side, as if a sentry once stood there.

Her heart pounded. She had walked these halls many times but had never registered this hidden route. Drawing closer, she realized the arch had subtle carvings, runes that half resembled the glyph on her wrist. The space beyond was dark, though a faint cold draft drifted out. She hesitated only a moment before slipping through.

Beyond was a narrow corridor that curved gently downward. Each wall bore small alcoves with empty stands. Perhaps they once held mirrors or relics. The dusty floor showed footprints, some fresh, some old. Hers now joined them.

She shivered, the realization sinking in that this must be a part of the Sanctuary that had been deliberately hidden. She thought of the missing seers, of the meltdown creeping through every corridor. Could Lucien have used passages like this to come and go unseen?

The corridor ended at a broad stone door that fit seamlessly into the wall. She almost missed it, since no handle was visible. A faint pattern of symbols dotted the center. She raised her flashlight, her breath catching at what she saw etched near the top. *IVY LEWIS*, spelled in spidery script. Beneath it, half-buried in a design, one small word glinted in the light.

End.

CHAPTER

TWENTY-FOUR

THE VISION SPLITS

Ivy's sleep felt uneasy from the start, as though the air itself pulsed with static. She had cramped herself into the corner of her small bed, arms wrapped around her knees, half expecting something to strike at her the moment her eyes closed. Outside, the city lights filtered through the thin curtains, casting restless shadows across the walls. She breathed in the faint aroma of burned sage Robin had wafted through the apartment earlier, but it did little to calm her. She sensed a coming storm in her mind, a turbulence more frightening than any physical threat.

She drifted at last, and almost immediately, her consciousness folded inward. Images sprang forward, bright and terrible. She saw city blocks illuminated by flames. Buildings groaned under the burden of smoke that blotted out the moon. People ran, silhouettes made of panic and confusion, as if stalked by invisible hunters. A wave of power, or perhaps raw fear, crackled through the

226

streets, knocking lamps dark and warping reflections in every glass surface.

Inside the dream, she stood motionless in the center of a fractured intersection. The asphalt had split open, revealing molten rock below. She heard the cry of seers, some she recognized from old gatherings, others unknown. They staggered through the haze, chased by intangible shadows. Each time one of them turned or stumbled, multi-colored sparks of power erupted. Those sparks vanished almost as quickly as they flared, leaving only ash behind. She watched with widening eyes, her heartbeat pounding in her ears. She tried to move her feet, to lunge forward and help them, but her body felt as though it weighed a thousand pounds.

A figure appeared at the far end of the ruined street. For a moment, she thought it was Ethan, tall and tense, calling her name against the roar of distant sirens. Then a red glint illuminated the figure's hair. No, that couldn't be Ethan. As she strained to look, the entire scene blurred, melting like a film strip burning in a projector.

Ivy found herself catapulted backward through darkness until she was standing on the roof of a skyscraper. The wind whipped her hair across her face. All around her, the skyline crumbled into gray dust. Bridges collapsed into the bay. The Golden Gate turned to a silhouette of black iron that slid beneath churning water. She gasped, stepping backward, wanting to close her eyes but unable to tear her gaze away.

Then the vision shifted. It felt as though her perspective split wide open. Sharp images overlapped. In one, Lucien stood beside her on that same skyscraper rooftop, his pale eyes fixed on the destruction below. He leaned in, almost as though he shared her horror, but there was no sorrow in his face. Instead, a look of triumph lingered at the corner of his mouth. In the other overlapping viewpoint, she stumbled through the chaos with Ethan's hand firmly gripping hers. Together, they pushed against the panic, heading for an arched portal of shimmering light. Water poured off the edges of that portal, as if it separated reality from something unknown. She could hear him shouting her name, but the wind swallowed the sound.

The dual visions began to warp her senses. Smoke bled into the bright glow of the portal, and both futures entangled in front of her eyes. Lucien's voice whispered, "You stand at the threshold." Ethan's voice shouted, "Hold on to me!" Each demand tore at her mind, each promise beckoned her with a different kind of power.

Her body felt like it might rip in two. She clutched at the glyph on her wrist, desperate to anchor herself, but it glowed with an erratic pulse, almost mocking her frantic attempt at control. No matter where she turned, she saw tragedy. Seers cowering in alleyways, illusions devouring real people as creeping flames devoured entire neighborhoods. She saw old acquaintances from the Sanctuary falling to the ground. She heard telepathic screams that shattered windows and left shimmering psychic shards in the air. The city was dissolving into ruin, but even that dissolution existed in two distinct threads.

In the first thread, Lucien lifted her chin gently and pointed toward the blackened skyline. His voice hummed through her consciousness. "The illusions are real if we let them be," he said, his eyes shining with cold certainty. "We can rebuild from ash, but only if you embrace what you are." She felt his hand move around her waist, pulling her closer as the skyscraper trembled beneath them.

In the second thread, Ethan squeezed her hand so tightly it hurt, his breath ragged against her ear. "Close the door, Ivy," he called out. Rugged determination lined his face, the dedicated reporter who never gave up on finding answers. Behind him, an eerie glow expanded, shaped like a doorway in the very air. She tasted salt and fire on her lips. Ethan's gaze turned urgent. "I can't do this alone," he pleaded. "You have to make the choice." Around them, smoke raked the sky, an inverted storm that threatened to seal them inside.

The two realities collided, jarring Ivy's senses. She felt a scream building in her throat. Everything that she tried to hold back, the guilt, the longing, the dread, all coalesced into raw terror. The streets below, the portal, Lucien's half-smile, Ethan's fierce resolve, the howling city, they overlapped until she couldn't separate them anymore. She dropped to her knees in the dream's half-formed landscape.

Smoke choked her lungs. Pain lanced her temples. She tried to blink, but the images remained superimposed, as though her mind had become a split mirror. One half reflected the path with Lucien, the other half the road with Ethan. She wanted to choose, to wrench free of the illusions, but every time she reached for clarity, a fresh wave of psychic static surged against her.

A fierce wind buffeted her, stinging her eyes with ash. She pressed trembling fingers to the ground for balance, half-certain she would fall through it. A kaleidoscope of lightning cut across the sky, revealing monstrous shapes that might have been illusions or something worse. She couldn't look away. Her heart hammered until she thought it would explode from her chest. She opened her mouth but no words formed. Only a scream rose, a primal outpouring of fear and anguish that tore from her throat as the two visions ripped at the edges of her consciousness.

She screamed again, and the cityscape split apart. Bridges crashed into the water. Streets fractured into broken mosaic. The entire world fragmented around her, and the chaos intensified, faster and faster, until it resembled a spinning top in her mind's eye. The kaleidoscope reached a blinding flash, white-hot and silent. No breath, no sound, no feeling.

Then she woke.

She jerked upright, gasping for air. Her chest heaved as she fumbled at the sheets tangled around her legs. Sweat beaded across her forehead, and her pulse thundered like she was still falling through that dream. She blinked rapidly, struggling to separate nightmare from reality. The overhead light was off. Only the faint glow of the street-lamp outside sliced through the curtains, illuminating the small bedroom.

At first, everything felt too quiet, like the moment after a deafening explosion when the ears refuse to process sound. Ivy sat still, her shoulders shaking as she tried to ground herself in the present. She stared at the bookshelf, the nightstand, anything that proved she was in a real, solid space. Her glyph still throbbed on her wrist, an echo of the pain she'd felt in the dream.

For a long minute, she listened for footsteps or a voice, maybe Ethan's, maybe Robin's, but heard only the distant traffic. When the dull roar in her ears subsided, she breathed out in staccato bursts, forcing her trembling limbs to still. Something glinted at the edge of her vision, and she turned her head. The nightstand had been empty when she fell asleep, but now it bore a single envelope.

Her heart lurched. She swallowed hard as she swung her legs over the side of the bed. The sheets slid to the floor in a twisted mess, but she barely noticed. A faint tang of wax teased her nostrils, mingling with the smell of her own sweat. She stared at the envelope, uncertain whether her eyes might still be trapped in the aftershock of that violent vision.

No illusions drifted across its surface, though. A thick, cream-colored envelope, sealed with a deep red wax stamp. She saw intricate whorls pressed into the seal, the same symbol she recalled from earlier confusions, an emblem that once marked a presence she couldn't name. Her hand shook as she reached out. The edges of the envelope felt real, the paper thick beneath her fingertips.

Close to the top edge, bold pen strokes spelled out the name that made her draw in a startled breath. *Mrs. Ivy*

Grey. She stared at the words, barely blinking, her heart pounding so loud she was sure the entire building could hear. Something primal fluttered in the pit of her stomach. She parted her lips, intending to speak, but found no voice.

THE STORY CONTINUES

The story continues in book three, **SEER'S VISIONS,** coming soon to Amazon.

EXCERPT FROM SEER'S VISIONS

Ivy jolted upright on the couch, the taste of smoke still clinging to her throat. In the vision she had just escaped, flames devoured the skyline while friends attacked one another, lost in twisted illusions. If she didn't stop Lucien's plan, that nightmare would become real by dusk. The glyph on her wrist seared with warning as she forced herself to stand. A single candle burned on the kitchen counter, she was sure she had blown it out hours ago.

Her shoulders tensed. Something had changed while she slept. She crossed the living room, brushing past piles of books and half-burned incense sticks. A low hum seemed to emanate from the corners of the space, an invisible resonance that prickled along her skin. She realized her glyph tattoo was growing warm, a gentle throbbing against her wrist. She rested a hand over it, hoping to calm the relentless rhythm. The city had been unstable for days now. The air hummed with stray telepathic waves, leaving seers sleepless and afraid. Ivy had done what she could to steady them, but it was never enough. Whatever message Lucien had sent, she needed to unravel it before the city burned. She rubbed her warm glyph, willing her nerves to settle.

As she made her way down the dim hallway, she spotted Robin in her bedroom doorway. She wore a dark sweater and threadbare jeans, the ends of her newly dyed purple hair curled around her collar. She looked up, eyes soft with concern.

"Ivy," Robin said quietly, lifting a hand in an awkward wave. "You're back. Good."

Ivy nodded wordlessly. She brushed her thumb across the scorching seal on the envelope, feeling the warmth break through the paper. At that contact, her vision wavered: dream images, glimpses of candlelit corridors and chanting voices. She pulled back with a startled gasp, her head spinning.

"Ivy?" Robin's voice was sharper now.

"I saw..." She pressed a hand against her temple. "Just for a second, I saw corridors like those in the Sanctuary. Voices chanting. It looked ceremonial, but there was something else too. An altar maybe. Or a space prepared for something big."

Robin exhaled, shaky. "He's drawing you in."

Ivy's heartbeat hammered. She squared her shoulders, determined to keep calm. "He can't force me to join that vision," she whispered. "I refuse to let him manipulate me the way he used to." She paused, noticing how close Robin was, how real her breathing sounded in the silence. "I'm not alone this time."

Robin's expression softened. "No, you're not."

They sat like that for several moments, letting the hum of the city beyond the windows fill the silence. Cars passed on the street below, a muffled siren wailed south of the neighborhood, and Ivy could almost pretend this was a normal afternoon. Except the letter in her hands made that impossible.

Finally, she lifted the envelope and turned it so both of them could see the address:

Mrs. Ivy Grey

The directness of it sank deep into her chest. She felt as though the letters themselves pulsed with each beat of her heart. If she looked away, she might lose the nerve. So, she kept her eyes fixed on the graceful script, letting the final illusions at the edge of her senses subside.

Robin placed a hand on her knee. "You don't have to open it," she repeated softly. "Not tonight. Not ever, if you choose."

Ivy gave a bitter little smile. "That's comforting," she said, "but I already know. Pretending ignorance won't save me, or anyone else." She brushed hair away from her damp brow. "If he's demanding a response, I can't hide from it. If I do, he wins by keeping me off-balance and afraid."

Robin swallowed, then nodded. "Then I'll stay with you."

Ivy managed a small, grateful smile. Despite everything crashing down, Robin's unwavering presence kept her from drowning in her own terror. She said nothing further, just placed a steady hand at the small of her back as if to lend her strength. She turned her attention to the envelope. The wax seal glowed under the lamplight.

Seconds ticked by with excruciating slowness. Finally, she slid her thumb beneath the seal. It cracked with a soft pop, as though releasing a breath it had held captive. Ivy's pulse spiked, but she pushed past the panic, unfolding the cream paper inside. And in that moment, she knew she had crossed a line she could never uncross.

She stared at the first words. Her name. Then a single line of text.

Across the room, Robin breathed in sharply, bracing for whatever she had to reveal. But Ivy's chest felt hollow. No date. No location. Only that simple, ominous message. For a heartbeat, she closed her eyes, her mind roiling. Then she looked up, meeting Robin's gaze. She read the dread in her expression and knew something had shifted.

Slowly, Ivy arose from the mattress, the paper trembling in her hand. Robin stood as well, still close by. Outside, the day's light began to slide toward dusk, painting the sky a brooding shade of gray. The quiet in the apartment thickened, an unnatural stillness that amplified every breath, every stutter of the candle's flame.

She turned the paper so Robin could see it.

The ceremony begins at dusk

Nothing else. Yet Ivy's heart pounded as though each syllable vibrated through her soul.

Robin exhaled. "Ivy, I..."

She trailed off, unable to finish. In that silence, the final illusions she had sensed at the edge of her vision suddenly snapped into sharper focus. She glimpsed lights in unknown rooms, shadows moving in choreographed unison. She heard faint chanting under. And she tasted the metallic tang of both fear and dangerous yearning. The faint smell of smoke and candle wax drifted around her, so strong that mentally she felt staggered.

She stood absolutely still, letting the letter dangle between her fingers. She had spent all this time dealing with half-formed glimpses, but this felt different. More certain, more immediate. Somewhere, Lucien was setting a stage and beckoning her forward, even though he'd never said her name aloud in that line, she felt his signature in every curve of the ink.

Something inside her locked into place: a single truth. She couldn't go back to ignoring her power, nor could she pretend that Lucien was merely a voice in her head. Reality had shifted around him, and with each vision, with each pulse of the glyph on her wrist, she had begun to step onto a precise path. Now he had extended the final invitation. And she understood, to her horror, that she might be the only one who could answer.

Ivy moved back to the bed, her knees weak. Robin curled an arm around her shoulders, offering silent reassurance. The candle on the windowsill sputtered, as though buffeted by an invisible wind. Outside, no horns blared. No voices called. The city itself felt like it was holding its breath.

She murmured, "I can feel it... the inevitability."

Robin's eyes glistened. "It's going to be okay," she whispered, though she sounded uncertain.

Ivy nodded faintly, though she didn't believe her. "I'll figure it out," she said, voice shaking with false conviction. "I'll face whatever he's planning."

She tangled her fingers in Robin's, taking a moment to breathe in something tangible: her warmth, her loyalty. She lifted her gaze to the envelope again, swallowing past the dryness in her throat. Perhaps she had always known this moment would come. Perhaps every pulse of her visions had led her here.

She closed her eyes, closed her fist around the paper, and finally exhaled.

CHAPTER ONE
THE ENVELOPE

Ivy jolted upright on the couch, the taste of smoke still clinging to her throat. In the vision she had just escaped, flames devoured the skyline while friends attacked one another, lost in twisted illusions. If she didn't stop Lucien's plan, that nightmare would become real by dusk. The glyph on her wrist seared with warning as she forced herself to stand. A single candle burned on the kitchen counter, she was sure she had blown it out hours ago.

Her shoulders tensed. Something had changed while she slept. She crossed the living room, brushing past piles of books and half-burned incense sticks. A low hum seemed to emanate from the corners of the space, an invisible resonance that prickled along her skin. She realized her glyph tattoo was growing warm, a gentle throbbing against her wrist. She rested a hand over it, hoping to calm the relentless rhythm. The city had been unstable for days now. The air hummed with stray telepathic waves, leaving seers sleepless and afraid. Ivy had done what she could to steady them, but it was never enough. Whatever message Lucien had sent, she needed to unravel it before the city burned. She rubbed her warm glyph, willing her nerves to settle.

As she made her way down the dim hallway, she spotted Robin in her bedroom doorway. She wore a dark sweater and threadbare jeans, the ends of her newly dyed purple hair curled around her collar. She looked up, eyes soft with concern.

"Ivy," Robin said quietly, lifting a hand in an awkward wave. "You're back. Good."

Ivy nodded wordlessly. She brushed her thumb across the scorching seal on the envelope, feeling the warmth break through the paper. At that contact, her vision wavered: dream images, glimpses of candlelit corridors and chanting voices. She pulled back with a startled gasp, her head spinning.

"Ivy?" Robin's voice was sharper now.

"I saw..." She pressed a hand against her temple. "Just for a second, I saw corridors like those in the Sanctuary. Voices chanting. It looked ceremonial, but there was something else too. An altar maybe. Or a space prepared for something big."

Robin exhaled, shaky. "He's drawing you in."

Ivy's heartbeat hammered. She squared her shoulders, determined to keep calm. "He can't force me to join that vision," she whispered. "I refuse to let him manipulate me the way he used to." She paused, noticing how close Robin was, how real her breathing sounded in the silence. "I'm not alone this time."

Robin's expression softened. "No, you're not."

They sat like that for several moments, letting the hum of the city beyond the windows fill the silence. Cars passed on the street below, a muffled siren wailed south of the neighborhood, and Ivy could almost pretend this was a normal afternoon. Except the letter in her hands made that impossible.

Finally, she lifted the envelope and turned it so both of them could see the address, *Mrs. Ivy Grey*, elegantly inked with a flourish. The directness of it sank deep into her chest. She felt as though the letters themselves pulsed with each beat of her heart. If she looked away, she might lose the nerve. So, she kept her eyes fixed on the graceful script, letting the final illusions at the edge of her senses subside.

Robin placed a hand on her knee. "You don't have to open it," she repeated softly. "Not tonight. Not ever, if you choose."

Ivy gave a bitter little smile. "That's comforting," she said, "but I already know. Pretending ignorance won't save me, or anyone else." She brushed hair away from her damp brow. "If he's demanding a response, I can't hide from it. If I do, he wins by keeping me off-balance and afraid."

Robin swallowed, then nodded. "Then I'll stay with you."

Ivy managed a small, grateful smile. Despite everything crashing down, Robin's unwavering presence kept her from drowning in her own terror. She said nothing further, just placed a steady hand at the small of her back as if to lend her strength. She turned her attention to the envelope. The wax seal glowed under the lamplight.

Seconds ticked by with excruciating slowness. Finally, she slid her thumb beneath the seal. It cracked with a soft pop, as though releasing a breath it had held captive. Ivy's pulse spiked, but she pushed past the panic, unfolding the cream paper inside. And in that moment, she knew she had crossed a line she could never uncross.

She stared at the first words. Her name. Then a single line of text.

Across the room, Robin breathed in sharply, bracing for whatever she had to reveal. But Ivy's chest felt hollow. No date. No location. Only that simple, ominous message. For a heartbeat, she closed her eyes, her mind roiling. Then she looked up, meeting Robin's gaze. She read the dread in her expression and knew something had shifted.

Slowly, Ivy arose from the mattress, the paper trembling in her hand. Robin stood as well, still close by. Outside, the day's light began to slide toward dusk, painting the sky a brooding shade of gray. The quiet in the apartment thickened, an unnatural stillness that amplified every breath, every stutter of the candle's flame.

She turned the paper so Robin could see it: *The ceremony begins at dusk.* Nothing else. Yet Ivy's heart pounded as though each syllable vibrated through her soul.

Robin exhaled. "Ivy, I..."

She trailed off, unable to finish. In that silence, the final illusions she had sensed at the edge of her vision suddenly snapped into sharper focus. She glimpsed lights in unknown rooms, shadows moving in choreographed unison. She heard faint chanting under. And she tasted the metallic tang of both fear and dangerous yearning. The faint smell of smoke and candle wax drifted around her, so strong that mentally she felt staggered.

She stood absolutely still, letting the letter dangle between her fingers. She had spent all this time dealing with half-formed glimpses, but this felt different. More certain, more immediate. Somewhere, Lucien was setting a stage and beckoning her forward, even though he'd never said her name aloud in that line, she felt his signature in every curve of the ink.

Something inside her locked into place: a single truth. She couldn't go back to ignoring her power, nor could she pretend that Lucien was merely a voice in her head. Reality had shifted around him, and with each vision, with each pulse of the glyph on her wrist, she had begun to step onto a precise path. Now he had extended the final invitation. And she understood, to her horror, that she might be the only one who could answer.

Ivy moved back to the bed, her knees weak. Robin curled an arm around her shoulders, offering silent reassurance. The candle on the windowsill sputtered, as though buffeted by an invisible wind. Outside, no horns blared. No voices called. The city itself felt like it was holding its breath.

She murmured, "I can feel it... the inevitability."

Robin's eyes glistened. "It's going to be okay," she whispered, though she sounded uncertain.

Ivy nodded faintly, though she didn't believe her. "I'll

figure it out," she said, voice shaking with false conviction. "I'll face whatever he's planning."

She tangled her fingers in Robin's, taking a moment to breathe in something tangible: her warmth, her loyalty. She lifted her gaze to the envelope again, swallowing past the dryness in her throat. Perhaps she had always known this moment would come. Perhaps every pulse of her visions had led her here.

She closed her eyes, closed her fist around the paper, and finally exhaled.

OTHER FLORID ROMANCE BOOKS

To be notified of new releases and special promotions from Florid Romance, please join our email list:

https://floridromance.lmbpn.com/about/sign-up-for-our-newsletter/

For a complete list of books published by Florid Romance please visit our website:

https://floridromance.lmbpn.com/

BOOKS BY KELLI ROBYNS

The Enchanted Orchard

The Orchard (Book 1)

Family Curse (Book 2)

Crystal Heart (Book 3)

The Charmed City

Spellbound (Book 1)

Prophecy (Book 2)

Ultimatum (Book 3)

Crescent City Curse

Beignets and Bad Omens (Book 1)

Moonlight and Muddy Waters (Book 2)

Queen of the Quarter (Book 3)

In My Mind's Eye

Oracle Project (Book 1)

Dark Dreams (Book 2)

Seer's Visions (Book 3)

BOOKS BY MICHAEL ANDERLE

Sign up for the LMBPN email list to be notified of new releases and special deals!

https://lmbpn.com/email/

For a complete list of books by Michael Anderle, please visit:

www.lmbpn.com/ma-books/

CONNECT WITH MICHAEL ANDERLE

Website: http://lmbpn.com

Email List: https://michael.beehiiv.com/

https://www.facebook.com/LMBPNPublishing

https://twitter.com/MichaelAnderle

https://www.instagram.com/lmbpn_publishing/

https://www.bookbub.com/authors/michael-anderle